Sometim
yourself that you don't want to know...

Seth drew back, wrapping his arms around his knees. Old girlfriends and guys he'd hung out with in the past flashed in front of his eyes, each one of them offering some piece of advice: *run away, stay right where you are, touch him, don't touch him, wake him up, let him sleep, tell him everything in the morning,* and *don't you dare say a word.*

It didn't seem right leaving Clay all by himself, but Seth knew he couldn't stay any longer. Carefully rolling off the bed so as not to wake the man up, he rummaged around in the dark until he found a folded blanket. He opened it up and spread it over Clay's body, carefully smoothing down all the wrinkles.

"Sorry," he whispered. "I'm just confused, that's all. You understand, don't you, Clay?" He swallowed hard. "I think I know your secret now. Never get drunk around me again, understand? I'm not ready to deal with this yet."

One last touch on Clay's foot, and Seth turned to leave the room. "You don't want me, anyway," he said softly. "I'm not good enough for you, Clay. What you need is someone who can really be there for you. Me, I can't even make up my mind about a kiss on the hand."

The Name of the Game

Torquere Press Novels

911 by Chris Owen • An Agreement Among Gentlemen by Chris Owen
Bad Case of Loving You by Laney Cairo
Bus Stories and Other Tales by Sean Michael
Bareback by Chris Owen • The Broken Road by Sean Michael
Caged by Sean Michael • Catching a Second Wind by Sean Michael
Cowboy Up edited by Rob Knight
Deviations: Discipline by Chris Owen and Jodi Payne
Deviations: Domination by Chris Owen and Jodi Payne
Deviations: Submission by Chris Owen and Jodi Payne
Don't Ask, Don't Tell by Sean Michael
Fireline by Tory Temple • Galleons & Gangplanks, editor Rob Knight
His Beautiful Samurai by Sedonia Guillone
Historical Obsessions by Julia Talbot • Hyacinth Club by BA Tortuga
In Bear Country by Kiernan Kelly
Jumping Into Things by Julia Talbot
Landing On Both Feet by Julia Talbot
Latigo by BA Tortuga • Locked and Loaded edited by SA Clements
The Long Road Home by BA Tortuga
Manners and Means by Julia Talbot • Music and Metal by Mike Shade
The Name of the Game by Willa Okati
Natural Disaster by Chris Owen
Need by Sean Michael • On Fire by Drew Zachary
Old Town New by BA Tortuga
Out of the Closet by Sean Michael • Perfect by Julia Talbot
Perfect Ten: A Going for the Gold Novel by Sean Michael
Personal Best I: A Going for the Gold Novel by Sean Michael
Personal Best II: A Going for the Gold Novel by Sean Michael
Personal Leave by Sean Michael • A Private Hunger by Sean Michael
PsyCop: Partners by Jordon Castillo Price
Racing the Moon by BA Tortuga • Rain and Whiskey by BA Tortuga
Redemption's Ride by BA Tortuga
Riding Heartbreak Road by Kiernan Kelly
Secrets, Skin and Leather by Sean Michael
Shifting, Volumes I-III, edited by Rob Knight
Soul Mates: Bound by Blood by Jourdan Lane
Soul Mates: Deception by Jourdan Lane
Steam and Sunshine by BA Tortuga
Stress Relief by BA Tortuga • Taking a Leap by Julia Talbot
Tempering by Sean Michael • Three Day Passes by Sean Michael
Timeless Hunger by BA Tortuga
Tomb of the God King by Julia Talbot
Touching Evil by Rob Knight • Tripwire by Sean Michael
Tropical Depression by BA Tortuga
Under This Cowboy's Hat edited by Rob Knight
Where Flows the Water by Sean Michael
Windbrothers by Sean Michael

This is a work of fiction. Names, characters, places, and incidents either are the product of the author's imagination or are used fictitiously. Any resemblance to actual events, locales, organizations, or persons, living or dead, is entirely coincidental and beyond the intent of either the author or the publisher.

The Name of the Game
TOP SHELF
An imprint of Torquere Press Publishers
PO Box 2545
Round Rock, TX 78680
Copyright 2006 © by Willa Okati
Cover illustration by Rose Meloche
Published with permission
ISBN: 978-1-60370-011-5, 1-60370-011-0
www.torquerepress.com

All rights reserved, which includes the right to reproduce this book or portions thereof in any form whatsoever except as provided by the U.S. Copyright Law. For information address Torquere Press. Inc., PO Box 2545, Round Rock, TX 78680.

First Torquere Press Printing: April 2007
Printed in the USA

If you purchased this book without a cover, you should be aware the this book is stolen property. It was reported as "unsold and destroyed" to the publisher, and neither the author nor the publisher has received any payment for this "stripped book".

The Name of the Game
By Willa Okati

Torquere
Press Inc.
romance for the rest of us
www.torquerepress.com

Chapter One

"What next?"

"Are we on the clock?" Anthony stretched luxuriantly, arching his back. His toes flexed and curled against the soft quilt he lay on. "You realize you don't have to stop what you're doing. I could go on like this for hours. Your hands…"

Clay skated his fingers up Anthony's slender legs and grinned, his smile made for doing wicked things in the dark. "I want to know. Everything he did, I want to do better. Come on. Teach me. Or don't you think I can learn?"

"You're already one hundred percent above his standards."

Clay chuckled. God, he loved teasing Toni. The game never got old. Besides, he had a certain standard to meet. "Oh, no, not good enough," he chided. "I have to be at least twice the man he was. Go on. Tell me what he did after that."

"He kissed me." Anthony tilted his head up. Clay moved with the flexing of his body and balanced above the man. He brought his mouth down to Anthony's, brushing lips across lips in a gentle, feather light touch. Anthony moaned softly when Clay's tongue flickered out, too briefly, he knew, to be satisfying. "More."

Anthony reached for Clay, angling for a kiss. The scent of Anthony, already growing aroused, spicy cologne and some woodsy body powder and man was a heady aphrodisiac to Clay's nose. It'd been a long, long time since he'd been with anyone who appreciated him the way Toni did.

Grinning to himself, Clay combed his fingers through Anthony's hair. "This is beautiful," he said, tangling the strands and then separating them out. "Sunshine color. The way the sun looks on rainy days when it's just coming out from behind the clouds."

Anthony licked his lips. "I'm a bottle blond."

"Oh?" Clay raised an eyebrow. "Do I get to find out for sure?"

"Play your cards right."

"What next, then? Keep on telling me. I have a memory to erase."

"Big, strong man."

"You bet. Go on."

"He touched me," Anthony said simply. "All over. He acted like he couldn't get enough. But he was fast, really fast. I wanted slow."

Clay lifted himself up into a kneeling position, braced on either side of Anthony's narrow hips. His hands, big and strong from the hard work he did, rested on Anthony's shoulders.

He began to massage them gently, digging in with the pads on his thumbs. "Like this?"

Anthony sighed, a soft ragged sound, and shifted with pleasure. "Oh, yes."

Clay moved on, skating down the soft skin and lean strength of Anthony's arms. "All this muscle… it shows that you work for a living," he murmured. "Did he touch you everywhere?" He hovered near Anthony's navel, circling it with one finger. "As in, everywhere?"

Anthony licked his lips, staring up at Clay through darkened eyes. "Everywhere."

"Like this?" Clay slipped his hand beneath Anthony's royal blue tank top, feeling his stomach contract as Clay's hand ran across it, up to his bared chest. Anthony shivered and made a low sound as Clay ran calloused fingertips across one nipple. "Easy, baby, easy. I won't hurt you."

"You could never hurt me." Anthony swallowed hard. "Next?"

"Next."

"His mouth. On me. Just there."

Clay teased with his fingers. "Where I am right now?" He moved, the fabric of the bed rustling as he bent down for one more kiss on the corner of Anthony's mouth. "Or here?"

"There," Anthony whispered. "On me."

"Then I've got to match him, move for move," Clay said. Gently, he pushed the dark blue fabric of Anthony's tank away from his chest. Palming the left pectoral, working it

lightly with a velvet and leather touch, he bent
down to first kiss, then nip at the swelling bud
of Anthony's other nipple. He sucked it briefly
into his mouth, lashing it with his tongue, then
drew the whole of the dark circle between his
lips.

"Oh, God!" Anthony moved beneath Clay,
tossing his head to-and-fro on the soft cotton
pillow Clay had given him to make sure he
was comfortable. "Clay. Fuck, Clay. Please."

Clay lifted his mouth away. "You like this?"
The sound of Anthony's quick breathing was
all the response he needed. Clay gave Anthony's tit one last hard kiss, then moved his
mouth away from it. "What next?"

"Fingers. All over me. Can you -- will
you?"

"I aim to please." Clay shifted, adjusting his
erection so that it rested against Anthony's
thigh. He gave Anthony another glittering
look. "Did he do this, too?"

"You're bigger. And better. Much better."
Anthony writhed against him. "More."

"Like this?" Clay swirled his hands over
Anthony's body. Wherever there was cloth, he
moved it aside. Going for improvisation, he
kissed wherever his fingers had gone, leaving a
trail of small red marks in his wake. He
tongued the small bruises down Anthony's
arms, across his lower belly, and then moved
to his thighs, so soft, yet hard with jogger's
muscles.

"You feel so good," he whispered. "This is better than anything I've had in a long time."

Anthony managed to laugh. "Whose fault is that?"

"Mine. I should have done this sooner." Clay had slithered down the length of Anthony's body. He crouched at his feet, holding out his hand, not quite making contact with Anthony's body. "Where else did he touch you?"

Anthony looked at Clay and grinned. "Where do you think?"

"I suspect the fact that you're still wearing your cutoffs is stopping me from going there."

"Is that all?"

"Anthony…" Clay stopped to breathe in and steady himself. "What next?"

Anthony laughed. "Either you go for the gold, or I hit you with a pillow for being such a tease. I'll be damned. The cliché is true. Best friends do make better lovers."

"Too bad you can't turn me into your knight in shining armor, baby." Clay bent down for one more kiss. He couldn't manage to hide his grin. "The way you look and move, Toni." He sighed. "If I weren't determined to preserve our buddyhood, I would so be getting lucky tonight."

Toni gave him a look he had seen on more than one bedmate's face: pure annoyance mixed with the good humor he seemed to inspire in most people. He jerked the pillow out from beneath his head and smacked Clay with it. Lightly. "Tease."

"Oh!" Dramatic, pretending Anthony had wounded him, Clay twisted and collapsed next to his best friend, laid out like a Christmas present on his bed. "I'm a goner," he said, hand pressed to his heart. "I've lost my touch with the menfolk."

Toni lifted himself onto one elbow. He lightly tapped his fist to Clay's nose. "You really are a jerk, you know."

"I wouldn't say that. I jerk off plenty, sure, but --"

"What about this?" Anthony gestured at his body. "You do a pretty good imitation of a man who has all it takes to get some." His gaze dipped lower, lingering over Clay's groin. "Is that a ruler in your pocket, or are you happy to see me? Friendship, huh?"

Clay shrugged and gave Toni a look calculated to annoy seven kinds of hell out of him. "I was picturing Brad Pitt."

"Oh -- you!" Toni pounced on Clay, tackling him with all his hundred and thirty pounds of hard, lean weight. Clay gave a loud *oof* sound before flinging his arms around Anthony and wrestling.

"I can take you," Anthony boasted, evading Clay's attempts to pin his hands. "You think you're man enough for me?"

"Thought I was twice the guy of your last date." Clay finally managed to subdue Toni, who lay laughing beneath him. The flush of arousal was fading from the man's cheeks, but Clay could still see his lips were swollen from their kisses, and feel how hard his nipples were. "Hey, hon. Did I go too far? I'm sorry if I -- well, you know what I -- I'm sorry. It was just a game."

"I know." Anthony reached up to caress his cheek. "You're a goofball. And a sorry loss for one-half of the population of this bedroom. Good news, though -- you wiped out the memory of that awful last date. And I can definitely pronounce you a Don Juan in bed." Anthony mimicked pressing a seal to Clay's forehead. "Anthony's Stamp of Approval. Absolutely guaranteed to give you the time of your life."

Clay touched his head. "Does that stay? Is it clear to the naked, gay eye? Will it get naked gay men to eye me?"

"It could happen."

"Dear God, please." Clay rolled off Toni, flopping down beside him. "I've been keeping company with my own hand for so long Mr. Happy is about to declare a moratorium on Rosie Palm and her five daughters."

"Rosie, huh? No wonder you wanted a sample, you tramp. You've been seeing six women on the side. About time for a little of your own kind."

"Yep," Clay agreed happily. He stretched himself, a good long arch from stem to stern, head to bare toes, as he burrowed down into the soft quilt. "Oh, hey, how do you like this? I got it on special at the hippie shop downtown."

"Jesus, which hippie shop?"

"The one where they serve you herbal tea and some kind of veggie biscuits if you spend enough." Clay stroked his bed cover approvingly. "They made this up themselves. Hand quilting. You just don't *get* that kind of handiwork anymore."

Anthony made a clicking sound with his tongue. "Yeah, you're gay. Aptitude in bed aside -- definitely gay."

"How gay?"

"Any more spin on it and you'd burst into flames." Anthony turned on his side and faced Clay. He ducked in quickly for one last kiss, pressing down hard. Lips were lips, and Clay couldn't help rising to them, moving back against Anthony's mouth.

Anthony drew away, grinning. "That's to remember me by. And one more thing. If I ever ask you to erase the memory of a bad one night stand from my mind, do it with tequila. I'd have more to regret the morning after, but this isn't exactly safe for either of us."

Clay felt his face warm. "Sorry," he mumbled.

"Don't you dare apologize. This was the best I've had in a long time. I'm not saying I don't regret the lack of a grand finale, but you? You're number one with a bullet." Anthony cocked his head. "So why haven't you been on a date in almost six months?"

"If I had a nickel for every time I'd asked myself that, I'd be a very rich man."

"Hmph." Anthony drummed his fingers on the quilt. "This is really nice. Crushed velvet? Silk? Linen? Bet they made this out of cast-off dresses. I'm going to steal it, just so you know. And by the way, we have to do something about finding you some action." His grin became predatory. "We, Sir Clay, are going to find you a date, toot sweet, and then we're going to work on me."

"I thought we just did."

"Do you want to get popped again?" Anthony made a threatening fist. Clay backed down, waving his hands. "Didn't think so. Good."

Anthony rolled across the quilt, displaying the curve of a toned ass which, Clay had to admit, would tempt any man to go for the home run. He opened Clay's bedside drawer, blinked for a moment, then burst into laughter.

"Hey, don't make fun of my buddies."

"God, how many friends does a man need? A gay man should have maybe two or three of these. Plus a butt plug. Possibly something double-headed if he has a playful type in his life. But this?"

Anthony reached into the drawer and pulled out a realistically-shaped dildo. He waved the penis at Clay like a snake. A very firm snake.

"Three, max. Not thirteen, of varying sizes, shapes, and from what I can tell, flexibility."

"You're giving me lessons on what I should have in my nightstand? You're a sex bunny who enjoys no lack of company. Maybe one cordless multispeed is all you want for those nights when you're alone, but --"

"No but. And no butts, either. Hon, this is just sad." Anthony tossed the fake cock down between them. It rolled sadly toward Clay like a lonely puppy in search of its master.

He petted it. *Ah, my trusty number nine. Gooood boy.*

"I wouldn't say that," Clay protested. "I could be out there like all the other lonely guys my age, looking for some company. Anyone with a cock works for those types."

"And this is a problem?"

"Well, not so much a problem, no." Clay pulled Anthony toward him, letting the slight man snuggle onto his shoulder. He tossed the dildo aside, although he made sure it didn't roll off his comfy mattress onto the floor. "You're young, cute, and hung. You have it easy."

"Easy!"

"Okay, okay. There's nothing about the dating life that's simple to deal with. I give you that point. But let's face it -- you have no shortage of men in your life. For one, you've got a buddy who's willing to cuddle and comfort you after really bad sex."

Anthony snorted, but instead of elbowing him, curled closer around Clay. "Yeah. Life wouldn't be the same without you." An idea seemed to strike. He angled his neck to look up at Clay. "Bars. Why don't you go to them anymore?"

"Eh…" Clay waggled his hand. "You've heard of what happens with me and cruising, right?"

"I've heard of your admiration for Tom Cruise."

"I should be so lucky," Clay muttered. "Okay. Back to the basics."

"Gay 101."

"Class is in. Here's your basic cruise: say, walking down the street. You see a really hot guy with ripped abs, a toned ass, fantastic legs --"

"Hey! No fantasizing about others when you have someone who fits the qualifications right here."

"You and I aren't meant to be, sweetie."

"I could buy you another toy and name it after me."

"It's just not the same."

"Damn."

Clay kissed the top of his friend's curly hair. "You gave it a shot. But okay, back to your basic cruise. You pass this hunka, hunka deli-cious love, but you don't know anything about him. Gay? Straight? Who can tell? It's not like we go around with pink triangle T-shirts." He shuddered. "Anyone I'd want to cruise back, that is."

"So? Keep talking, Professor."

"Well, hopefully you make eye contact as he passes by. Wait to the count of three, maybe four, then stop and look back. If he's stopped, too, and he's looking at you, you might just be in for a rockin' good time."

"Pretty much the way I understand the game. Sounds simple." Anthony nudged his chin into Clay's chest. "So why don't you just go for a lot of long walks?"

"Who walks anymore now that they have this newfangled thing called a horseless carriage? Ow!"

"You deserved it. Okay. Back to my original point. Why not cruise at bars?"

"Because you don't notice it, being too busy getting snapped up by the first young thing that spots you, but for a guy like me a gay bar looks like a track meet. Everyone's walking around in circles, desperately cruising every single guy in there. You could go cross-eyed from everyone giving you a look."

"And? I'm failing to see the bad part."

"Huh. Either you really do get snagged right away or you haven't been in a gay bar in a while."

"It's been a few weeks. I only go with you, and for the past while you wouldn't go with me."

"Honey, my little queen, I'm glad to have you hang out with my thirty-something self. Other men might not be so understanding. The last thing I want is to fight over you."

Anthony sulked. "That's not fair. You're denying us both the pleasure of eye candy. Everyone's just so gorgeous in those places!"

"Stereotyping. Shame on you; you should know better. You know what it's like to be a human gay man. We are definitely not all perfect tens. We're just guys, like everyone else. Fat, skinny, tall, short, hairy, smooth, toned, tubby -- more flavors than ice cream. And the ones cruising the bars, well..." He shrugged. "They're just like me, except maybe more so. All of them lonely. Looking for Mr. Perfect. That isn't what I'm in for. I want someone who wants me back for a reason, not because I have a fantastic ass."

"It is pretty remarkable. And I know asses." Anthony gave Clay's hip a playful pinch. "Fine, walks and bars are out. What about parties? I know you've talked about that underground club downtown."

"Too many drugs, and too much booze. Not a happy combination. Then you have circuit-walking cruisers who are stoned *and* drunk. Alas, my dear," he said with a melodramatic sigh, "I am doomed to walk this life alone, with only my Friend of Dorothy card in my hand for company."

"Yeah, and your cock in the other one. Wanking yourself down the drain because you'd rather lie here and whine instead of doing something about it." Anthony shifted until he was lying on his tummy with his forearms supporting his weight. His perky ass jutted up in a way that would have been enticing if Clay hadn't thought of Anthony as the next closest thing to a younger brother.

Alas, Clay thought again. *Darn you, inherent nurturing qualities.* Still. He couldn't change what he felt, not that he'd want to try, games aside.

Did Toni have a point, though? Maybe. But no matter how much fun he made of the "meat" and greets he was apt to find in the gay lifestyle, he did want to find someone special. Unique. Tailor-made just for him.

Trouble was, he'd been searching for a while, and he'd come up dry.

When in doubt, turn to a smart woman. Failing that, a queen would do nicely. Clay had learned his lesson about that a long time ago. He smoothed his hand down Anthony's back. "Okay, then, O Wise One," he teased. "You have a better idea? I'm all ears."

Anthony frowned for a moment. Then his eyes lit up like a string of lights on a Christmas tree. "Uh-oh." Clay shifted back. "I've seen that look before, and it never ends well."

Anthony grinned like the Cheshire cat who'd just stolen a whole shelf full of cream bowls. He followed Clay, nuzzling his chin into Clay's ribs. "I have," he said, "A Plan."

Clay could hear the capital letters, and they made him nervous. He moved uncomfortably on his quilt, suddenly too warm. The soft, cream-colored walls of his room, decorated with Spanish hangings and pictures of exotic beaches, plus, hey, a few cartoons, seemed to press in on him. He licked his lips. "Do you want to elaborate on this plan?"

"Oh, I will. Anthony's here, he's queer, and he knows a thing or two about the ways of lo-o-o-ve."

"Talking about yourself in the third person is a sign of insanity."

"Dork." Anthony sat up and stretched, yawning -- all without losing his smile. "Come on. Feed me, and I'll fill you in on everything."

"Are you blackmailing me?"

Anthony arched a look back over his shoulder. "Don't think of it like that. Call it bribery. You make me a sandwich, and I lead you straight to the hottie of your dreams."

Well, when the guy put it that way… Clay sat up and scooted off the bed. He still felt plenty nervous, as he'd been on the receiving end of Anthony's Plans once too often, but the gleam in his eyes piqued Clay's curiosity far too much to say "no".

"All right," he said. "One sandwich. Then you tell me how I end this lonely existence and find a hot stud to wrap myself around like a hot, tight Slinky."

"Deal."

Well, Clay thought as he followed his best friend out of his bedroom, *if nothing else, this should definitely be interesting...*

Chapter Two

Clay entered the kitchen not entirely of his own free will. He had a small but determined locomotive force behind him, name of Anthony, pushing him along every step of the way.

"I don't want to do this. Jeez, you're strong! Come on, Toni, have a heart."

"I do -- a big one. That's why I've decided to give you a little help getting past your recent dating slump. I love you too much to let you be alone."

"Could you love me a little less and let me schlep along without interference?"

"Nope!" Anthony declared cheerfully. He maneuvered Clay into a sitting position at the kitchen table, which actually only pretended to its status.

Clay admired the thing for a moment. True male innovation. He'd furnished his half of the home on the tenet of "the curb giveth, and the curb taketh away". People threw out the most amazing stuff. Sure, he could have afforded to go to a fancy chain store and gotten the latest in neo-modernism, but it was the principle of the thing.

After all, he was a bachelor, albeit a gay bachelor, and he had certain standards to live down to. The kitchen table was actually an old desk with two mismatched chairs drawn up to it. A third, made of folding metal, leaned against one corner for when Anthony came over to eat, usually when he'd cooked -- which wasn't often. Clay lived on takeout when he could get it, and nuked the odd meal when he couldn't.

Still grumbling as he allowed Anthony to push him down into place, Clay protested: "I have got to say, this clocks in as one of your worst ideas ever to date, full stop, exclamation point."

"Your grammar and punctuation need a little help. Make a note." Anthony steered Clay into precise position just as if he were a painting that needed to hang a little straighter. So to speak. "It's not like this is a big deal, Clay. Lighten up. Plenty of people have tried online dating. I hear it actually works for a lot of them."

"Obviously, you haven't tried the online chat rooms," Clay retorted. "If I went in there looking for love, I'd be faced with the derision of a third, obscene offers from another third, and the final third with nothing better to say than claiming they have nine-inch cocks."

Anthony looked fascinated. "For real?"

"Oh, ye innocent. These guys measure from the back crack of their asses to the tip of their tall tales. Show me a cock that long in nature and I'll show you a guy who's making a killing in porn films, or possibly a genetic mutant."

Anthony sat down across from Clay, leaning his chin on one slim hand. "Tell me more. This is fascinating."

"Well, they --" Clay stopped. "I know what you're doing. You're taking notes on what kind of man does and doesn't do it for me, so you can put down every detail and trivial pursuit factor in this online ad you're determined to make me create."

Anthony shrugged without a trace of guilt. "And you have a problem with this?"

Clay regarded his friend glumly, pouting. "I'm not going to win this argument, am I?"

"Nope."

"Okay. Fine." Clay gave in as gracefully as he could. "One condition, though. You can log on, you can find me a good-looking site, but then you have to read what's out there. Then you take a good hard second to think about whether or not you want to subject me to their tender mercies."

"You make yourself sound like a piece of filet mignon someone's about to throw to a junkyard dog."

"I' faith, you have come close to the truth. In fact, you've hit the target dead center." Clay tried to wiggle out of his chair once again. "Come on, this is really a bad idea. Let's go get some ice cream --"

"At this time of day?"

"Okay, coffee then. Big hot double espresso for you, something with mocha and cream for me, and --"

"You're never going to get any *cream* unless you sit your ass down and start typing," Anthony stated sternly.

Clay's cheeks heated. Geez. You'd think that as a man who'd been out and proud for over ten years, a little frankness from a twink wouldn't affect him.

That was Anthony, though. Clay loved him like a brother. An annoying, bratty, pushy kid brother who always wanted to play. Still, though, there was the affection. And he didn't get enough of that to turn Anthony down, nor did he, he glumly admitted, have the intestinal fortitude to stand up for himself when Anthony had his heart set on something.

"I'm typing, I'm typing," he grumbled as he dragged a small laptop from the far end of the desk. It'd been covered in newspapers since the last time he'd ventured online at home and found a bald eagle web cam. After watching the feed for over an hour, he'd realized he was in desperate danger of becoming a complete geek and switched the machine off.

Now, at work, he was online all the time. Looking up facts, trivia, news of the weird, you name it. He knew his way around the Internet like no one else at the radio station. Good thing, too. All those tired afternoon workers depended on Clay, the hyperactive DJ, to keep them awake during the drag-time shift -- and he delivered.

"I don't see those fingers moving."

"I have to open the computer and boot it up first." Clay shot Anthony a playful glare. "Brat."

Anthony nodded and began to hum, tapping his fingers as the laptop revved into action. When he heard the beep that signaled Clay tapping into an online connection, he squealed and dragged his chair around to Clay's side. "Let me at those keys!"

Clay surrendered control gladly. As Anthony navigated, Clay leaned back to watch him. The man had a head for business, he had to say. As part-time manager at a spa that specialized in unique hours for unique clients, he had the savvy, the smarts, and the inner strength to make his life work like a dream.

They made a point of meeting after their shifts ended, often going out for a meal or retiring to one or the other's apartment. It was rare that they came to Clay's, as Anthony swore up and down that the place brought out his inner Martha Stewart -- someone he tried to keep well squashed down. "Next thing you know I'll be decorating with macaroni and gilt leaf," he'd said once. "The earth would rotate backwards and we'd all be flung off into space. Clean up or shut up with the invites."

But today, Anthony had been all for coming back to his place. Ah, if Clay had only known the man had a secret agenda on his mind…

Beep. Beep. Click, click, click. Beep!

"Found you one," Anthony announced proudly, surrendering the keyboard to Clay. "Check this out and see if it doesn't hit all your hot buttons."

Resigned, Clay dragged his attention to the dating site Anthony had picked out. At first glance, he had to admit it wasn't bad. No flashing banner ads, no promises of "pearly pink pussy" or "rock hard cock" with interesting pictures to match the neon words. Nice and calm, discreetly and professionally done, and definitely a man's site with its dark shades of green, blue, and brown. "Okay, points for finding a needle in a haystack," he had to concede.

Then, he read the logo at the top. "You have got to be kidding me."

"What? It's perfect for you."

"Welcome to Fairyland," Clay read out loud. "A place where gentlemen can be pretty, witty, and gay. Copyright pending." He gave his friend a dark look. "Anthony…"

"Just give it a chance," Anthony insisted. "Go ahead, pull up a few profiles. See what's out there."

"You really want to see? Fine." Clay clicked. "Okay, here's Gerald, age thirty-nine. Gerald, as you will notice, loves to work out, go on five-mile runs, and cook nouvelle cuisine."

"And? What's the problem?"

"Gerald, as you will also notice, is pictured as sitting behind a desk so we can't see the results of all that exercise or, quite possibly, the potbelly from eating at diners. The man has arms like a limp spaghetti noodle in a baggy shirt. Please interest yourself in the fact that Gerald is also bald except for a creative attempt at a comb-over, and if he's thirty-nine, I'll eat the hard drive on this thing."

"You don't think?"

"Anthony, come on. The way he's grinning, his dentures are about to fall out."

"Okay!" Anthony raised his hands in temporary surrender. "So Gerald's a bust. Try someone else."

"Somebody say bust?" The front door opened into Clay's small kitchen. His housemate, Seth, stepped through, popping a motorcycle helmet off his head, then wriggling out of a leather jacket. Clay glanced from Gerald to Seth, from Seth to Gerald, then back at Seth, and felt the familiar wobbliness in his gut that heralded: *honey, he's home.*

Seth. All six feet two of him, well-packed into it with hard, lean muscles and an ass that wouldn't quit. Arms powerful enough to wrench off the most stubborn of pickle jar lids. A scent of smoke and the outdoors clung to his skin. As he headed for the fridge to pluck out a bottle of water, Clay watched and felt his own mouth go dry.

Seth, he thought wistfully. The man he lusted after, and the one he'd have tried to grab up a long time ago except for one little problem: the man happened to be straight. Not just straight, but arrow-like. Ruler-like. Whereas Clay was straight as a Slinky. Seth wasn't homophobic, but Clay wasn't stupid. There could never be anything between them.

If wishes were horses, though, he thought, returning to his computer screen with a glum sigh.

"There had better not be anything in this house worth running a bust over." Seth pressed the cold bottle of water to his forehead. "I just spent the night doing an undercover prostitute sting. Let me tell you, I have seen more T & A than I would have watching the scrambled porn, and every last bit of it illegal." He grinned -- that heart-stopping smile that made Clay's heart stutter -- and dropped loosely into the spare seat. "So, what are we doing?"

"Nothing," Clay said at the same time that Anthony helpfully chipped in, "Hunting online personals."

Clay covered his face with one hand as Seth, predictably, cracked up. "You're joking."

"Nope." Anthony gave Seth a cheery smile. "You know how long it's been since Clay was on a date. I'm giving him a helping hand. Never give up and all that. Seems to me that if he can't find someone on the street, okay, not *on* the street, Mister Cop, but in real life -- why not try the virtual world?"

He patted Clay's laptop. "I found a great site, too. Except someone won't give it a chance." A sharp nudge to Clay's hip reminded him again as to who wasn't playing fair.

"No kidding. Huh." Seth played the bottle across cheeks that had to be warm from the rising beachfront heat he'd ridden through when the sun came up, then opened the bottle and took a long sip. Watching the man's throat work, Clay thought, *hosanna and hallelujah.* "What's up with those sites, anyway? I thought they were all Spam wizards or something."

"They are." Clay aimed at a random listing and clicked. "Now, here we have Frank."

Seth angled his neck to look. "Frank isn't too bad -- from a straight standpoint."

"I grant you that he seems to be a fine, up-standing sort of character," Clay allowed. "However, read his profile."

Anthony leaned his cheek on Clay's shoulder. "Thirty-five, athletic, enjoys fine dining and long walks along the beach at sunset. Click here to send him an expression of interest." When Clay and Seth burst into laughter, he looked up, honestly confused. "What?"

"For one thing," Seth pointed out, "Have you ever actually walked on a beach after it's dark? Hello, jellyfish heaven."

"And don't forget shells."

"Plus the fact that it's about the biggest dating ad cliché on the market." Seth raised out of his chair and clapped Anthony on the back. "I think you might have to figure out some other way to give Clay a hand." He stopped to waggle his eyebrows.

Anthony, bless him, smacked Seth on the ass. He jumped forward. "Jesus, you're strong!"

"So I keep telling him." Clay scanned a few more ads, then shook his head. "Anthony, no. I can't do this. We'll have to figure out another way."

Anthony raised his hands. "Fine. White flag. Just pass over that computer so I can keep searching while you and Seth do that male bonding thing. You never know! I could find something really good, and wouldn't you be sorry if you'd missed out?"

"How would I know?"

Anthony gave Clay a narrow look. "Keep your logic out of this, and leave the computer wizardry to me."

Clay and Seth exchanged glances of: *Queens. What are you gonna do?* before Seth grinned and emptied his bottle. The phone rang as he was tossing his bottle toward the recycling bin. It bounced off.

"Would you grab that? This is probably for me," Seth said, reaching for the portable unit. He made a face. "Sophie, making sure I'm home in one piece."

"She still have it in for your motorcycle?"

"With a vengeance." Seth grimaced, then raised the phone to his ear and clicked it on. "Hello, Seth of Seth & Clay here -- hey, Sophie, good morning. Are you calling from work?"

He winced. "Yes, I was careful on my way home. Sophie, come on, I'm with the P.D. You think I want to get pulled over? No, I could not get out of a ticket with some kind of buddy handshake. The law is the law." Seth restrained himself with a visible effort. "Look, let's not do this right now, okay? How's your morning been so far?"

Anthony nudged Clay in the ribs. When he turned to the man with a questioning look, he made a devil's face with a sadistic grin and raised eyebrows. Clay elbowed him. "Cut that out," he whispered.

"What?" he retorted. "That's Sophie, right? What better way to show my love for the torment -- I mean, true love -- of Seth's life?"

Clay gave Anthony a light shove. "Back to your typing."

Anthony shook his head and began navigating again. His long fingers neatly used the mouse pad to scroll through text and clicked on first this, shaking his head, then that. Clay admired his technique even as his mind strayed to Seth.

Seth of the lickable abs, the bitable ass, the kissable lips, and the utter, total unavailability of his fine self. Aw, hell. Even if there had been a prayer of something between them, Sophie would have put a stop to it.

"Damn it, Sophie, no!" Seth raised his voice to bark. "I did not put myself in danger last night. I do what the Chief tells me. That's all. What? A prostitute sting." Pause. "Oh, for God's sake, no. I did not sleep with any of them. Well, of course I flirted, how else was I going to -- stop that, Sophie. Just stop. None of them meant a thing to me, and I cannot believe I'm having this conversation just after getting off the night shift. I'm tired, Sophie. Lunch? I'm going to be *asleep.*"

Clay sighed. Turning back to Anthony, he copied his earlier grimace. Anthony nodded in sympathy. A good guy like Seth needed to catch a break. Clay figured they both agreed that Seth deserved someone a whole lot more sympathetic to his situation, appreciative of his job, and less demanding of an account for every minute of every day.

All the more reason to regret... but nah, he wasn't going to waste any more time on what ifs and maybes. Clay returned to the computer screen, watching Anthony whiz through negatives and positives, each potential source neatly bookmarked in the browser for later perusal.

Suddenly, something caught his eye. "Wait, hold up. Go back." He leaned forward, peering at the screen. "Not that one. Yeah, the one before this. I want to take another look."

"Speed dating?" Anthony raised an eyebrow. "Clay, you're losing your mind. I put that one in the 'reject' list."

"No, no. This is interesting." Clay tugged the laptop closer to himself and folded his arms on the tabletop, settling down to read. "This doesn't look half bad, actually. You get to meet the guys in person. One-on-one."

"For all of fifteen minutes."

"Maybe you can take longer if you want. It doesn't say, but I bet so." Clay pointed. "Twenty dollars per meet, okay, ouch, but at least it's face-to-face. No need to wonder what good old Gerald is hiding beneath his desk. If they're hot and we can exchange a few decent words, then I can decide whether or not to risk a date with them. If they're not, then out with one and in with another."

Anthony wrinkled his forehead. "And this appeals to you?"

"More so than anything else you've come up with." Clay scrolled down the page. "And hey, look here, they have a center in town, near the beach."

"That's hardly surprising."

"In town." Clay nudged him with an elbow. "I can ask for morning or early afternoon meets. Won't have to worry about missing any work time. Maybe I'd hook up with someone

who works the seven to eleven, and not someone who works at the 7-11."

The men on the site didn't look half bad,
either. Even if they were paid models, the
company knew how to attract men. Only some
mild cutesiness about their tagline: "High
Speed Connections - For the Beachfront Single
Who'd Like to Roll a Double."

Not *too* precious. Just nasty enough to make
Clay grin in appreciation. "This is the one." He
tapped the mouse, determined. "I'm going for
it."

Anthony shook his head. "I really hope you
know what you're doing."

"Ah, come on." Clay grabbed him in a one-
armed hug. "It's all thanks to you. I'd never
even heard of this gig before. Sounds pretty
sweet to me." To prove his point, he pressed a
kiss to Anthony's temple, just below a row of
curls. "Good as my best boy here."

Anthony wriggled a little, then settled in
with a contented sigh. "Everyone should be so
lucky as to have a buddy like you in their life,"
Clay murmured, rocking them a little.

"Damn it! No!" Seth snapped, startling
them apart. "Sophie, would you just -- you're
at work. I don't care if you do have your office
door shut, language like that is going to get
you into trouble."

Clay and Anthony exchanged troubled
glances. "How long until he dumps her?" Anthony murmured.

Clay shook his head. "He won't. She's got him pussy-whipped."

"Clay!"

"What? It's true. Why else would he go back day after day? And let me tell you, when she deigns to grace this house with her presence, it's like a royal visit. She's got Seth wrapped around her little finger like a corkscrew, and we'd best not forget it."

"Fine! Don't call me during the day, then. I'm taking the phone off the hook. Got it? Good." Seth clicked his cell phone closed and winged it across the room. Clay managed to catch the projectile in mid-flight before it shattered into little pieces on the opposite wall.

"Problems?" Anthony ventured into the awkward silence that followed.

"Christ." Seth sat back down and rolled his head into his arms. "You find anything yet, Clay?"

"Speed dating," Anthony jumped in. "Fifteen minutes in a booth with a potential prospective. If you like them, you move on to the next level. Up to five candidates per day. Twenty bucks a guy for the company's fees, but Clay here is willing to pony up." He gave Clay's shoulder a hearty slap. "Anything for love, right?"

"Oh, yeah." Clay reached out and laid a hand on Seth's arm. A casual touch, nothing more than one guy would do for another when he'd clearly been vocally throttled by his lady love. "Sophie giving you a hard time again?"

"You have no idea." Seth's voice was low and full of misery. He raised up a bit to peer at them. "Say... do any of those sites have advice for getting rid of someone who's glued themselves to your side?"

The phone rang. They all ignored it. The sound had a Sophie-aura around the peals, and no one was that brave -- at the moment, not even Seth. The woman was a hell of a powerhouse, and woe betide anyone who stood in her way. Clay wouldn't put it past her to actually pay a visit to the house, but there were always locks -- and he'd be sure to throw all the deadbolts when he got a chance.

"I would suggest a beer, but it's too early," he joked, hoping it would get a smile out of Seth. The gratification he felt when his gambit succeeded brought an answering grin to his own face.

"You know, you've got it easy," Seth said after a moment. "Being gay. Someone like Sophie would never have sunk her claws into you."

"Should I thank you or be insulted?"

"Be grateful."

"For a woman who thinks gay people should be eradicated from the face of the earth?"

Seth pulled a face. "Yeah. It's one thing, her being a bitch to me, but you've never done a thing to deserve it except be yourself."

"The one thing she can't stand above all other things, including snags in her pantyhose and loose threads on her designer blouses."

"Gay."

There followed a moment in which Clay could hear two minds busily turning. He jerked upright. "No. I know what you're thinking, and no. Uh-uh. Not gonna happen."

"Aww, Clay," Seth purred, sliding his chair closer. "What, have I lost that indefinable allure?"

Clay swallowed roughly. *Like you said, you have no idea.* "This is all going to end in tears, Seth."

"You don't even know what we're planning yet!"

"Call it ESP. You're going to pretend you've jumped the fence to get Sophie off your back. Aren't you?"

Seth and Anthony exchanged innocent looks. The perfect 'who, us?' expression, and it fit right on the face of two cats with feathers dangling from their mouths.

"Would you excuse us for a second?" Clay asked. Seth shrugged, removing his arm from Clay's shoulder and standing up. He meandered out of the kitchen, probably heading for the bathroom.

Once he was out of earshot, Clay turned to Anthony for help.

"Don't," he said in a whisper. "Anthony, you know -- I can't -- don't do this to me."

Anthony's gaze turned soft. "Clay, honey, it may be the biggest favor I ever do you."

"But to lie about everything. Where's that going to get me except sitting in a bar with my heart broken, crying into my beer?"

"Tequila shooters."

"Whichever."

"Clay… trust me on this, all right? You can still do the speed dating. Just give your friend a hand."

"Yeah. Thing is, I want to give him more than a hand, and you know it. Pretending he's my lover just to get a woman off Seth's back? This goes farther than you've thought about, Toni. What if the guys on the force find out, and they think it's for real, too?"

"There are other gay men in the police, Clay. You're just being difficult."

"Got to admit Anthony's right," Seth startled them again by drifting back in to say. He leaned against a counter, soft waves of blond hair falling into his face. Looking at the man, Clay felt his heart give a double-thump. What he'd have given to be able to get up on his feet, cross over, taste those tempting lips in a sweet kiss, run his fingers through Seth's rumpled locks, stroke his back with the other hand…

"It isn't right," he finally managed. "It's not fair to -- you."

Seth shrugged. "The guys on the force don't like Sophie, either, not after what she did at the latest Policeman's Ball."

"Was that when she -- with the lobster -- and the prime rib -- and the chicken?" Anthony wanted to know.

"Oh, yeah. And the critiques of what the Chief's wife was wearing. The loud commentary didn't win her any friends. In fact, it made her a few enemies." Seth shrugged. "I figure I tell the guys about this, and they'll understand."

Clay started to feel cornered and outgunned. God almighty. It was like having a chocolate cherry cordial dangled in front of his mouth and not being permitted to take a bite.

But on the other hand… how could he say no? Even the chance of pretending to have Seth as his own had to be better than nothing, and it'd be as close as he ever got to the real thing. So, with Anthony and Seth's expectant gazes fixed on him, Clay gave in. "Fine," he said. "I'm in."

Anthony squealed and hugged Clay around his neck. Seth's eyes warmed with affection and good humor. He reached down and gave Clay a hug. "You won't regret this," he promised. "Sugar."

Clay couldn't get mad at Seth, or stay annoyed for long. He squeezed back, not letting himself linger on the play of muscles in the man's shoulders. "Nah. How could I not want to help a friend out?"

"Good," Seth said -- and without any warning, turned them just so, came closer, and kissed Clay on the lips.

Clay froze. *Whoa! Hold on, back up, circle the wagons. What the -- how the --* "Seth!" he sputtered as he broke free. "What the hell?"

Seth was staring at him. The faintest flicker of something dark and hot shone in his eyes for a moment before it was gone. "To seal the deal," he said awkwardly. "I figured, given the circumstances, it'd be better than a handshake."

Clay resisted the urge to raise his hand and touch his lips. What he'd longed to have for ages had been given without a second's thought. "Didn't the Romans finish off their bargains this way?" he joked to cover his roiling thoughts. "Maybe the Greeks?"

"Possibly Italians." Seth settled down into his chair. The strange look, whatever it had been, was wholly gone from his face. He leaned forward expectantly. "So, you're going to teach me all about what it takes to be a gay man, right? I mean, the whole nine. Clothes, mannerisms, cruising --"

"Whoa!" Clay raised his hands, laughing. "It's not like there's an initiation ceremony. You are, or you aren't. Just saying it is enough to make people believe you. Have you ever doubted I was gay?"

Seth considered it. "No, actually. Not since the moment I was interviewing potential housemates and you said 'By the way, I'm gay, hope that's not a problem?'." He grinned. "Hasn't bothered me yet, and now, it's going to help pull my nuts out of the fire. Just keep it up until Sophie is out of the picture, and then we go back to normal."

"Normal. Right."

Seth beamed. "You're a true friend, Clay. You know that?"

Once again, you have no idea. "Okay," Clay said, tilting his chair back. "Operation Exterminate Sophie has begun. This is the way we start…"

Chapter Three

Okay, so, brain… you want to let me know just what the hell happened in there? Seth frowned to himself as he shut the bathroom door. Habit dictated that he leave it open, letting the steam billow out into the house and sending Clay into a hissy fit -- good old-fashioned teasing -- but just then, he wanted the thing closed.

Fact one: he'd just kissed a guy.

Fact two: the kiss-ee had been his housemate.

Fact two-B: his housemate was gay.

Fact three: he'd kind of li… *whoa, there, brain. Retreat and regroup.*

Seth juggled the figures around in his head a few times, but always came up with the same conclusion -- he was screwed. Aw, man. The idea had just been a way to get rid of Sophie, the Siren who was Sucking Out his Soul. He'd never intended it to go even this far on the physical level.

Why, then, had he gone and kissed Clay?

As kisses went, it hadn't been anything to write home about, barring the "male" factor. *No, really, it wasn't,* Seth insisted to himself. A nice kiss, sure. Dry but gentle, almost tender.

Not the wet, squishy smack he'd planned on, or the backup dry peck he'd had as a contingency plan. It'd been a regular smooch, the kind he'd have given a… good friend. Who happened to be male. Who happened to be gay.

Seth prided himself on being a decent guy. A clean-nosed cop, even if he did have to get down and play dirty in Undercover. He liked his pranks, and when a relationship was headed for the Dumpster he'd do what it took to get out with his skin intact, but he didn't lead people on.

More, he had two eyes in his head. He'd seen Clay watching him. Always from a distance, very politely, never closing the gap between them on the gay-straight equator. He'd always known that if his bread were buttered on that side, Clay would have made a move right away.

There'd always been that nice, safe distance, though... That was, until he went crashing through it, lips first, and threw everything out of whack.

I seriously don't know what was going on in my head at that moment, Seth admitted to himself. He just prayed Clay would take it in the spirit intended, like the advanced form of a handshake, and not read in any further meaning.

He shrugged, rolling his shoulders. No reason to worry, really. He knew Clay about as well as anyone on the face of the earth, his

buddies on the force included, and he was sure
of one thing: Clay wouldn't go all starry-eyed
over a single kiss.

Sure, he'd been going through a dry spell
lately, but those happened to everyone. Clay
seemed happy with his life as a DJ and as long
as he had Anthony around, his good mood
stayed intact. Sometimes, Seth wondered if he
should have a talk with Toni and see if he
could swing Clay's pendulum for a while.
Close as they were, it'd probably do them both
a world of good.

He winced. *Right. A little more misogyny,
and I'll make chauvinist pig. Nice going, Seth.*
Being a cop didn't lend itself to developing a
boatload of sensitivity. If a man wasn't careful,
it made him hard as nails, inside and out. He'd
seen too many of his brothers on the force go
down to the bottle or worse, get picked up by
Vice themselves. One of the reasons he'd been
glad to have Clay around.

Clay helped him believe that he could be a
good man, a better man, and gave him a reason
to keep on fighting -- because he had friends
closer than family to come home to.

He shouldn't have done anything to risk
screwing that up. Jesus, he hoped Clay would-
n't be mad.

A shower would help clear his thoughts.
Shaking his head, the longish blond strands
flying into his face, Seth wrinkled his nose and
thought about how much he ached for a trim

and cut. No deal, though. Regulation didn't work for someone who did the regular stings. Long hair could be frizzed out, tied up, braided, tucked under a cap, whatever. His face wasn't exactly John Doe Brown, but he could blend into a crowd in a place like Vegas. Built, lithe, and compact. The kind of man who could spring into action, or be a fine candidate for a good time.

He knew he was good at his job. Units put in special requests to have him assist. He'd even been on a couple of cop shows, with his face blurred out and voice distorted, talking about what it took to dig deep and shovel up the things men tried to keep hidden in the dark. Sounded bleak, but Seth loved every second of it.

Except the hair. He could definitely lose the hair, and he wouldn't cry a single tear over it.

Reaching into the shower stall -- no tub, one of the many reasons Sophie had always refused to spend the night -- Seth turned on the water and cranked the lever all the way to scalding. Exactly how he liked the stuff. After a long night, he needed a good hot soak to get the sweat and grime off him. He'd never be able to hit the sheets smelling like he did, of motorcycle from his ride, smoke from the clubs, and a splash of bourbon to make his drunk act convincing. Cheap stuff, too.

As the water warmed up, Seth stripped off his clothes, one layer at a time. First the T-shirt, that had definitely seen better days. He half-laughed as a hole under one sleeve tore substantially wider when he peeled it away from his body. Who else got to shop for their work clothes at the Goodwill?

Jeans next, worn old and soft and thin as tissue paper, cut to cling to his legs and ass. Next day, he'd probably be in chinos to hide every bit of what he'd been showing off.

Seth tested the water. *All in a day's work.* The jets seemed hot enough, so he stepped in, closing the glass door and surrendering himself up to the blissful blast of water.

"Oh, yeah," he moaned. "Right there. Power shower, you are my friend."

Eyes closed, Seth reached for a bar of soap. He frowned when his fingers didn't encounter a familiar green brick, but instead found empty space. "Where the -- aw, man." He'd used the last of his good old store-brand soap the day before, after another stinky night in the beach's underbelly.

Damn. He could either get out, dripping all over the place, or he could borrow Clay's soap.

Seth peeked suspiciously at the cake resting in Clay's niche on the shower wall. He wasn't sure where Clay bought the stuff, but he felt pretty sure in guessing it didn't come with a logo stamped in the center and a paper wrapper. It looked almost… gummy. Felt that way, too, when he prodded the lump with one finger.

He could wash himself off with shampoo, but the feeling just wasn't the same. Nothing beat a good bar of soap, and this was nothing like a good bar of soap. This was some New Age contraption devised to confound men like himself.

But then again, he didn't think Clay would mind, so…

Seth snatched the bar up and began to apply it to himself. Good, even strokes up and down the ridges of his stomach, over the muscles in his chest, and across the shoulders. He peered anxiously at the trail of suds the bar left in its wake. Weirdly gritty, with a scent that made him think of breakfast for some reason.

A tentative prod at the skin beneath a cloud of foam made him blink. Damn, that was smooth. Seth had always been pretty hairless, but this stuff made him soft as a baby's butt.

Wonder if that's why Clay always kind of shines…

Back up again, brain.

Seth shook his head and carried on washing, considerately avoiding running the bar over any objectionable areas. More soap on a washcloth took care of the situation. Feeling clean at last, he put the bar down and breathed in deeply. Yeah, something food-like about the smell of the soap, not that he minded. This was how Clay smelled, and Anthony was always all over him, cooing about how he was good enough to eat.

Anthony, man… Seth relaxed against the shower wall, unconsciously running his hands over his chest. He wasn't his type, of course, being male, but the guy was a peach and no doubt about it. A cascade of curls, big wicked eyes, a curving mouth, and, when he got his drag on, breasts a man could happily smother in.

Knowing, however, that Anthony would bean him with a frying pan if he lingered too long over those kind of thoughts and he ever found out caused Seth to move on pretty quickly.

Mentally going over one pretty face led him to another, and Sophie slipped into Anthony's place with way too much ease.

Seth let himself sigh as he rubbed his soap-slicked belly. The woman would have been perfect. Hell, he'd thought she was a dream come true when they first met. The kind of up-town girl old Billy sang about, complete with blonde hair and blue eyes and a sweet, sweet smile.

Unfortunately, he'd found out that the outer Sophie had absolutely nothing on the inner Sophie, who should have gone around dressed in sharp icicles and prickly porcupine quills. Nothing had ever been good enough for her; he'd tried, God knew he'd tried, but he never had managed to satisfy the woman.

Do this, don't do that. Wear this, don't you dare wear that. Take me here, take me there.

Find another job, get yourself on the fast track to head up the force.

He could have handled anything if she'd left Clay out of the equation. Sophie had drawn herself up so tight and prim when she'd found out Seth roomed with a gay man, he'd half thought she was going to explode. Seth would let a pretty lady lead him around by the dick and pussy-whip him into submission, but he didn't stand for anyone tangling with his friends.

That'd been where the whole idea to get Clay involved had originated. Sophie plus her hatred of homosexuals plus her loathing for Clay would equal an immediate breakup and, carrying the one, leave Seth himself wide open to start playing that luscious field again.

Sex. God, sex would be wonderful. Seth didn't cheat, and he'd been celibate for weeks now with Sophie on a "good girl" kick. Apparently, she thought not giving anything up would make him crawl after her on his hands and knees, willing to give her whatever she wanted just for a little taste of something.

Seth snorted. He'd been doing plenty of crawling, thanks, but not for the sex. He didn't mind a woman who wanted to do her own thing for a while -- hell, it added to the mystery. Never knowing when you might get lucky kept a man on edge. More, it gave him time to get a better feel for the woman in question. He could learn her moves, her motivations, her morals.

And in Sophie's case, they had all totaled up to result in a money-grubbing, tight-fisted, bigoted bitch. Seth hadn't even wanted to have sex for a while now.

But when she was gone... Seth chuckled and ran his hands over his body with a little more purpose. That soap of Clay's seemed to cling to his skin, leaving it soft and supple. Even the thin trail of hair leading down to his cock was smooth and slick, like a strip of sealskin. And at the end of the road -- oh, yes.

Seth grasped his cock with a practiced movement, sliding one hand down the length and up the shaft. He handled himself loose and easy, getting a feel for the situation. As hoped for, he was ready to ride. Everything in an upright, locked position, slick from soap and hot from the shower water.

Thoughtful, he slid his thumb around the fat purple head a few times, wondering what he should choose for the object of his fantasies. Every guy had a selection of filmstrips in his head, just waiting to unreel at the slightest cause to drop a reel. He wound through old girlfriends, quickly discarding them because, after all, he hadn't said the final goodbye to Sophie yet.

Sophie, then? Seth considered the notion, then put it aside. He didn't need to get all mushy over the woman, not knowing what she was made of and how she treated the people he cared about.

He tipped his head back against the shower wall, letting his mind drift. The water would last for ages -- they'd invested in a huge tank, since both Seth and Clay were merfolk under the skin. Seth shut his eyes again and stroked his cock idly, letting his thoughts disassociate and run freely around until he was caught by a pair of brown eyes shining at him, warm with humor and sparkling with lust. No face to go with them, but Seth could work with a little flotsam and jetsam.

Focusing on the vision of those eyes, Seth ran a thumb up the underside of his cock, tracing each marbled vein with agonizing slowness. Just a little sting, exactly the way he liked his hand jobs. A little pain made the pleasure all the sweeter.

Sophie never had understood as much. Then again, if she'd had her way he would have been strung up by thumbscrews, dangling from his toes, and have a leash around his cock, so best to leave her out of the picture and focus on Brown Eyes, huh?

Seth couldn't remember where he'd seen them before. One of Anthony's soft-core "art films" that he and Clay could sometimes be caught watching? They were wide and innocent, with a lush depth fit to get lost in, surrounded by thick dark lashes.

It felt like a betrayal of Sophie, but Seth went with it. He couldn't have stopped himself by then. All the same, he tried focusing on the pure pleasure of the way his hand moved up and down his hard shaft, the way the skin stretched and rebounded over the steely core, and the little thrills of ecstasy that sent thin strings of pre-come bubbling out his slit.

Slowly, hazily, he brought another hand down to cup and roll his balls. Poor things couldn't decide what to do -- drop down and get cool in the heat, or rise up tight against his body in preparation for the payload.

Brown Eyes popped into his mind again, along with a wide, warm smile, and Seth groaned. He kept the face at a mental arm's reach, only letting himself focus on the vague memory every now and again as he took his own sweet time. Sophie had never done this willingly, and the few times he'd had her hand around him she'd had a moue of distaste on her otherwise kissable lips. Like he was dirty or something.

Well, he was. A raunchy man when it came to sex, and a good guy the rest of the time. Sophie didn't seem to grasp the distinction. She was like a book of riddles that he couldn't ex-actly manage to unravel, even with his head for figures. And speaking of figures... but nope, nah, Sophie was in the past, right where she belonged.

Seth caressed himself again, nearing the limits of his patience. Brown Eyes blinked at him, sweet and patient. God, he wished he knew who those orbs belonged to. At that moment, he'd have chased down their owner and begged for a chance to share a drink with them.

Pumping his own cock, setting up a steady rhythm, Seth sought for the answer to the riddle of where he'd seen those eyes before. He didn't think a movie, not anymore. This was someone he'd met. Someone he knew pretty well…

As if it had been summoned, Seth felt the orgasm he'd been waiting for rise up and tie knots in his belly. He flashed on the brown eyes again, and this time they had a face to go with them. A face that was handsome, not pretty, with a mop of tangled black hair and a square jaw.

"Oh, shit! Clay!" Seth yelped, and then he was coming harder than he had in years. Jet after jet of semen shot over his hands, spilling down over his member and his legs, thick and sticky and -- *oh, my God, I was fantasizing about a man!*

Seth leaned against the shower wall and heaved a huge sigh. God. Clay would never forgive him. He just prayed no one had heard -

The shower door flew open. Seth swore as a huge cloud of steam billowed out. "Jesus, that's cold! Don't just barge in a on a guy like that, you -- oh."

Sophie stood in front of him, impeccably dressed in a white linen suit, hands on her hips and, on her face, a look any sane man would have run screaming from.

"Hi," Seth attempted, leaning forward to try and snatch a towel. "Look, uh, Sophie, I'm not sure what you just heard, but it -- I --"

Hey, dummy! Seth's brain chimed in. *Use this to your advantage!*

Sophie was drawing herself up for an explosion, putting her hands on her hips and planting her tiny feet hard on the bathroom floor. Seth could tell she was winding up for a real showdown; he'd witnessed more than his share over the months they'd been going out. "Sophie, I'm sorry," he said gently. "Let me get a towel, and we'll talk, okay."

"Talk?" she sputtered. "I don't need to *talk*, Seth."

Not that she'll let that stop her, Seth thought wryly.

"This shower door?" Sophie rapped on it with her knuckles. "It's not as opaque as you might think. I saw you, what you were doing in there. And I heard what you said." Her lip trembled, which would affect Seth more if he didn't know she practiced the maneuver and hadn't seen it used on himself more than once. "Clay, you said. You called for him when you

-- you --" Her lip wibbled. "Seth, how could you?"

Seth gave up on waiting for her to clear out of the way, and shut the water off. He reached past one immaculate shoulder for a towel -- Clay's, he noticed -- and wrapped it around his waist. "I'll explain everything," he soothed.

For all her faults, Sophie was a lady, and he didn't treat women with disrespect. Intention-ally. Off the job. *Oh, God.* Seth shook his head as he stepped out.

She did let him pass; he gave her credit for that much. Deciding to forego toweling off his hair, Seth leaned against the bathroom counter, folded his arms over his chest, and gave her what he hoped was an honest look. Not a hos-tile one; he'd gotten past all that. He was tired of her attitude, her demanding nature, and her games. He felt weary and knew he probably looked the part.

"Sophie…" he started.

Her nostrils flared. "Clay. You said his name. That abomination you live with. It was him you were thinking about, weren't you? What, were you imagining him in there with you? On his knees, doing God knows what?"

God might know, but you sure don't -- or you don't share. Seth mentally slapped him-self. Breaking up with Sophie wasn't about the sex, honestly it wasn't. She didn't have a heart to give, so they had never really been in love.

All that remained between them were some messy details to sort out.

He'd go with the truth. Why not? Might be embarrassing later, but he wouldn't lie to the woman. "Yes," he said. "I was thinking about Clay." *And heaven help me if Clay ever finds out.* "I'd been doing what you said. Imagining him being in there with me." He felt his cheeks color red with embarrassment. "Sophie, beautiful, I'm sorry."

She quivered with outrage. "You should be sorry." One hand came up to cover her breastbone. "This is going to change things between us, Seth."

Seth braced himself. "How so?"

"Well -- well -- for one thing, you're moving out of here." Sophie took up an aggressive stance, one calculated to make the strongest man alive go running for his momma. Even Seth quailed a little bit, and he'd faced down drug dealers in his time. Five foot nothing with some blonde hair on the warpath and he could feel his testicles trying to climb up inside where it'd be safer.

She nodded decisively. "We're going to look for a new place today. I'm not having you around Clay anymore. He's a bad influence."

Ah. Now, time for the lies. Seth winced internally before saying: "Sophie… you're not making me move. I like it here." Truth so far, but then… "Sophie, do you want to sit down for this?"

Her chin came up. "I'm standing right here until you tell me what's going on. Either you're with me or you're against me, Seth. Now, are you going to get dressed and come with me or not?"

Seth sighed. "Not," he said softly, watching her face. It took a few seconds for the fact that she'd been denied to filter through. Sophie's expression became colored deep red with shock plus growing outrage. "I'm staying right here, because this is the place I want to live. This is where I can be myself."

"And that is?" she demanded.

Seth crossed his fingers where Sophie couldn't see them, tucked into the curve of his arm. "Gay, Sophie. I'm gay."

She blinked. "You're not."

"Honey, I think I'd know."

"Don't you 'honey' me! Of all the -- I have had some brush-off lines in my time, but this one beats them all, Seth."

"It's not a line."

"The hell it's not! You -- in the shower -- oh." Sophie's eyes dropped to the knot in Seth's towel. He saw her swallow. "Oh," she repeated, with a world of meaning in her voice. "Oh."

As she went pale, Seth flinched in alarm. He'd wanted her to leave, not have a coronary in his bathroom! Out of habit, he reached for the woman, trying to ease her back into a more comfortable position. "Baby, don't. Breathe, okay? Just breathe."

Sophie might have said something next, but Seth missed it in the explosion that was her tiny, powerful fist slamming into his chin. He swore, skidding with wet feet on the bare floor, and went ass over teakettle onto the tiles. White noise filled his head for a moment, and static burst into his ears.

When things cleared up, he realized he was staring dazedly at Sophie while she ranted on with the mother of all rants. "-- if I'd known for just one second that Clay would corrupt you like this, I'd have had you out of this hellhole months ago. Go ahead, admit it! That filthy fag and his nasty little friend have corrupted your mind!"

Seth shook his head, dazed. "No," he tried to say. "It isn't like that at all. Clay is…"

"What?" she demanded. "A friend? Something more? Your lover?" Her face had gone purple with rage. She kicked at Seth's unprotected genitals with one slim pump that came complete with a wicked heel.

Seth yelped and got out of the way just in time. His towel came away as he stood up. "Clay means more to me than you'll ever know," he said honestly. "He's special. You won't ever get it, Sophie, because you can't broaden your horizons beyond Channel WASP."

"He is your lover, isn't he?" Sophie's hands had balled into fists.

"You want to know what he is to me? Fine!"

Stomping out of the bathroom completely naked, Seth headed for the kitchen. He left wet footprints behind him he knew he'd have to mop up, but at the moment he couldn't have cared less.

He could hear Sophie hard on his heels, her shoes clicking a staccato beat as she tried to keep up. She was haranguing him about something, but he didn't bother to listen to what. He was headed for the man who'd always treated him like a brother -- not a cop, not a rung on the ladder, not a sugar daddy -- just a guy.

Clay and Anthony were still sitting at the desk-cum-table, their shoulders a little hunched and their cheeks pink. Seth spared a moment of regret for their embarrassment, and felt a new surge of anger against Sophie, who *still* hadn't stopped talking about abominations and desecrations and all other sorts of charnel-house crap.

"Clay!" Seth barked, pulling up short to the desk. "Stand up." When Anthony gave a slight squeak and Clay stared at him with confused eyes, Seth took matters into his own hands -- literally. Grabbing Clay by the lapels of his shirt, Seth hauled the man up onto his feet, tangled both hands in his dark hair, and pressed a kiss to eyelids he'd been daydreaming about, albeit all unknowingly, in the shower, and then on his soft lips.

Clay stood stock-still at first, unmoving as a statue. *Come on,* Seth prayed. *Get with the plan, bud. Do it for me.*

Slowly, although it seemed as if he was questioning Seth's sanity, Clay's mouth began to move. Seth let himself sigh out loud as he sank into the kiss, savoring it for what it was -- a piece of friendship that meant more to him than any of Sophie's cold caresses.

Then, he stopped thinking entirely. *Damn,* Clay knew how to kiss. A firm tongue came out to trace Seth's lips, moving around in a small circle, probing at the seam that held them together. Unconsciously, Seth opened up to let Clay in. It felt -- normal. Natural, the way a good kiss should develop.

With warm lips under his own, Seth groaned and shifted his grip on Clay until he had the man by the waist, drawing them into a closer contact. Clay went with him every step of the way, nestling in as if he were meant to be there. There was no trace of weirdness or uncertainty, but instead a sense of coming home. Seth felt *right* kissing Clay.

"Guys?" Anthony's voice intruded tentatively. Seth started away from Clay's lips just in time to hear a door slammed with an almighty thud. "Um, guys? She's gone. You can, er, stop now."

Seth looked up sharply to see an absolute lack of Sophie. He licked his lips and cleared his throat. "What did she -- did she say anything?"

Anthony shook his head. "Nothing I'm repeating." He pretended to look downcast for a moment before a twinkle sparked to life in his eyes. "You think she's gone for good?"

"Sophie? No way. She's just regrouping." Seth squeezed Clay again, giving his friend an easy shake. "Hey, I'm sorry about mauling you. I just couldn't listen to her ranting about you being a bad person. Not when you're one of the best I've ever met."

"Uh-huh," Clay said, looking dazed. "Seth?"

"Yeah?"

"You're naked."

"Lord have mercy, my virgin eyes!" Anthony jumped up and ran out of the room.

Seth ran his tongue over his lips again. "Say what, now?"

"You're really, really naked." Clay's throat worked as he swallowed. "And I don't know how to say this to you, but hey, I'm gay, you're male, you're naked, and I think we have a problem here."

"Oh, shit!" Seth jumped back -- right into the towel Anthony was holding out. He turned around, risking flashing him, and secured the terrycloth around his hips as fast as he could.

A few extra folds at the front, and with a mostly-turned-around stance, he looked back over his shoulder at Clay. "Hey, I'm sorry about the kiss."

"No." Clay waved him off, still looking stunned. "It was part of the act. I get it." He half-laughed. "I'm sorry, myself."

"Don't be. We're guys, things happen." Seth hitched his towel. "Look, I'd better…"

"Yeah." Clay sat back down. "You'd better."

Seth bore the weight of Anthony's gaze flicking back from one to the other of them for a full ten seconds before he got the hell out of his own kitchen for the second time in one morning.

Sporting a hard-on he could have pounded nails with.

Once around the corner, Seth careened to a stop and rubbed his face with his free hand. He loaded all the factors into his mental calculator and decided that he'd come full circle.

He truly was screwed.

And worse, he'd screwed around with Clay.

So far the score was: Day 2, Seth 0. What the hell would happen next?

Chapter Four

Clay stood in front of the bathroom mirror, checking himself over for the nth time. Was he ready to go? Hair carefully bed-headed, yup; teeth brushed? Yup. Nothing said 'potential disaster' worse than a piece of rice cereal stuck to an incisor.

Clothes? He spread his hands wide and glanced down, giving himself the once-over. One lightweight hoodie in a snazzy hunter green shade. One pair of jeans broken in to the shape of his body. Not a bad body, either, he hoped.

And the face? Boyish. Friendly, like a puppy ready to play fetch or chase its own tail for a change. He couldn't change the physiognomy, so might as well use it to his advantage.

He tried out a charming smile.

"Hi, I'm Clay. Good to meet you."

No.

"Hey, how's it going? Clay. Is what they call me."

No.

"Hey, have a seat. So we meet at last."

No.

"What's a nice guy like you doing in a place like this?"

No.

"Argh!" Clay grabbed his hair and tugged. "I'm never going to get this right," he earnestly told his reflection. The man in the mirror nodded, agreeing: he was doomed to make an ass out of himself.

Groaning, Clay leaned down over the counter and rested his head on folded arms. Nothing could go simply, could it? First Anthony and Seth had concocted their devilish scheme to drive the Ice Princess screaming into the night. He'd have been able to handle the plan. Had almost convinced himself of it.

Then, Seth had upped the ante by planting one on Clay that nearly knocked him off his feet. Only the two strong arms around his waist had held him upright, pulled into an embrace better than he'd felt in months. No, better than ever, because it was Seth, and it had been a dream come true -- until Sophie had left and Seth had backed down.

Their shower had gotten a hell of a workout that day. Seth had used all the hot water, but Clay hadn't minded. Cold did wonders for his state of mind and the state of his persistent erection.

Had Seth felt it, pressed against him? Surely he must have. Clay had tried breaking the news to him gently, but he wasn't sure if it was his careful wording or Sophie's departure that had caused Seth to jump away.

If it had all ended there, he'd have been satisfied. Sophie gone; good. No more games.
But uh-uh, Seth was still determined to go the
full nine. Clay was going to have to teach him
everything there was to know about being gay.
He'd even thrown in the trump card of having
to learn a new skill for Undercover. Someone
who could play the role convincingly would be
able to penetrate -- Clay winced -- a whole
new rank and file of crimes.

So, had he had a moment to himself in the
past week? Not a one. When he wasn't working, Seth had immersed himself in reading
Clay's magazines and asking questions.

"What's it like when two guys sixty-nine?"

Oh, God. Clay had moaned, feeling his
cheeks heat up. For a worldly-wise guy, Seth
could be so naive at times.

"You mean there's a Kama Sutra for gay
men?"

Clay had thumped his head lightly against
his forearm. Seth didn't know, or Clay hoped
he didn't, how his questions affected Clay. The
big head struggled for answers that wouldn't
send his housemate screaming into the night,
while the little head popped up eagerly and
wanted to demonstrate.

He thought he'd handled things pretty well,
though. The status quo between them had almost returned to normal, and no one could
have been more relieved. Hence this morning's
jaunt. Seth was giving Clay a lift to the speed

dating place in a local strip mall, dropping him off on his way to the gym.

Ooh. Gym. Sweaty muscles.

Hey, down, boy, down!

Outside, someone leaned on the car horn. "Hey, Clay!" he heard Seth bellow. "Come on! I'll miss my chance on the best machines if you don't get it in gear, and I mean fast!"

"Coming!" Clay yelled back out of the bathroom window. He slid it into place with a thump, took one last look at himself in the mirror, agreed with his own expression of mingled hope and despair, and got out before Seth decided to leave him behind.

He went out of the door with a quick check to see if it had locked behind him and then slid into the passenger seat of Seth's car. Clay stole a glance at his driver, who was occupied with drumming his fingers on the steering wheel in tune to an edgy rock beat. Wisps of honey-blond hair had escaped his short ponytail and fanned down around his cheeks. Bright green eyes focused on the driveway in front of them as he hummed along.

Oh, yeah, speed dating, here he came.

Anything to take his mind off the dichotomy of a man he was supposed to pretend to love, but had to keep to a hands-off policy with. It had to be better than this.

Seth turned to Clay, his grin dazzling as always. "Ready to burn rubber?"

"For a cop, you sure drive like a bat out of the hot place." Clay reached hastily for his seatbelt. "Do me a favor, huh? Don't get me killed on my way to meet the stud of my dreams."

"Do my best." Seth put the car into drive and pulled forward, putting his foot down the instant they were out on the open road. One hand flicked out to jack the volume on his stereo, blasting the car with sound.

Seth threw his head back and whooped in delight. "Get the motor running, head out on the highway," he sang. "Looking for adventure --"

Clay couldn't hold back a grin a moment longer. Ah, hell. Whatever came of this crazy scheme to hold Sophie at bay, he'd never stop thinking of Seth as a one-hundred-percent friend. You couldn't not love the guy.

"Rock and roll," he agreed, and rolled his own window down to let the wind whip through his hair as they sped down the hilly beach roads.

* * *

When they pulled up to the strip mall, Clay read the tasteful sign above the small unit with a gulp of nerves. Looked deserted except for a small red-haired woman sitting at a reception desk and a few tasteful chairs.

Beside him, Seth frowned. "You sure this is the place?"

Clay checked his directions, then glanced at the marquee again. "Appears to be. So, I'll meet you back here in about an hour, hour and a half?"

Seth narrowed his eyes, tapping on the wheel. "Actually…"

"Oh, no." Clay held his hands up. "I know where you're heading, and don't go there. I do not need someone holding my hand through this. I had to talk Anthony down from being my personal escort just so he could cop an eyeful."

"No, seriously, Clay, come on." Seth turned to face Clay. He had his own puppy face on, which, while being endearing, looked more like a tenacious German Shepherd's expression. "I think I should go with you. Where else am I going to find out what it's like when two gay men hook up?"

"Oh, yeah. That'll be great. Me with my bodyguard in his tee and short shorts? The guys will really think I'm available then."

"Clay, be a sport." Seth pushed him lightly. "I'll stand in the background. Be unobtrusive. I can do it, you know I can. Give me a chance."

"Absolutely not. No way." Clay shook his head. "Stop giving me the look. It won't work."

"Clay, please."

"Not playing fair."

"All's fair in love and war."

"Yeah, and so is bashing the enemy across the head with a great big stick. Seth, you are not coming in with me."

Seth paused, then turned the car off. He pulled the keys out of the ignition and flashed Clay a wicked grin. "Stop me."

He was out of the car before Clay could recover enough to undo his own seatbelt. "Seth, no!" he yelped, untangling himself. "Seth, stop!"

Too slow. By the time Clay had fumbled his way out, Seth was already inside, charming the petite redhead with his best smile. "…here for the five-thirty appointment," he finished saying. Apparently spotting Clay, Seth waved him over. "And here he is, the man himself."

The redhead turned her best 'receptionist' smile on him. "And you would be Clay McPherson, correct?"

Clay eyed her up and down. He struggled to hold back a smile. Not too prominent, but the Adam's apple was there, and for such a small 'woman', she had darned big hands. She caught him looking and her eyes began to sparkle. "Jeri at your service," she said, shaking his hand. "You've got good instincts."

Clay couldn't help chuckling. "Me? I'm nothing. Now you, you have the look down to an art form."

"Oh, go on," she said, waving one manicured finger at him. "Now. It's only been a week since you applied, so we only have one candidate for you today. Hey, hey, no sad faces. It usually takes about a month for the names to circulate and build up a decent level of interest. Besides," she said, dropping her voice to create the image of confidentiality, "someone cute as you is bound to snap up a prize right away. Could be tonight's your lucky night!"

Clay gave a mental shrug. One week in, so he supposed he should be glad anyone had nibbled at the bait at all. "Lead me to him," he said, finally letting go of the receptionist's hand. "Is it a back room, or…?"

"A small cubicle, over to the side there by the third ficus. You've just missed one rush and beat the second one, which is why the place looks empty right now." She beamed a dazzling smile at them. "And will your, er, friend be accompanying you?"

The last was spoken with an air of mixed hope-he-will and hope-he-won't. Clay stifled another grin. Looked like Seth had won himself a new groupie. From the look on Seth's face, he was halfway between appreciation and panting with his tongue hanging out.

"He's coming with me," Clay decided. "Seth, we're going walkies. Into the room over here -- this one? -- and you get to check out some more gay men."

"Can we talk later?" Seth asked the redhead. She nodded, lips curving into a perfect Cupid's bow. "After my friend gets through with his, er, speed date."

"Seth." Clay tugged at his arm. "Come on. I think there's something you need to know."

"I do?" Seth turned away from Jeri the Luscious and focused on Clay, good-natured again. "What do you mean, more gay men?"

Clay whispered into Seth's ear.

The look on his face made the whole bodyguard role entirely worthwhile.

* * *

Jeri's sweet voice floated in on the intercom. "Clay, are you ready? Your date is here."

Seth, leaning against the wall, sulked. "I still can't believe she is a he."

"Believe it," Clay retorted. He turned to Seth. "How do I look?"

Seth, bless his heart, didn't get thrown by the question. He studied Clay carefully before rendering the verdict: "Messy, but cute. I like the gold earring."

Clay touched the small hoop in his ear and smiled. "A gift."

"From Anthony," they said together.

"Who else? He dragged me into the piercing parlor a few months back. Normally, I just wear a tiny titanium stud you'd barely notice. Tonight, I figured I'd go for the pirate look. Pretty snazzy, huh?"

"Shiver me timbers." Seth laughed. "Come on, let's get this over with. Then, how about you and I head out to a bar?"

Clay felt a warning tic beneath his left eye.
"Depends," he said carefully. "It's kind of
early. What type of bar?"

Seth shrugged. "The sort you'd hang out at."

"Seth, I don't exclusively hang out at bars
where the men are all about the men. I like a
quiet beer in a normal hetero establishment
just fine."

"Okay, all right. I would like to go to a gay
bar," Seth clarified.

"Why the hell do you want to do that?"

"Because!" On Clay's eye-roll, Seth grudgingly explained. "I want to see what it's like
out there. I mean come on, Clay, this is a
whole new world. Men who look like bomb-
shells, good enough to fool even me, and guys
like you? I have got to see what this is all
about."

"Seth, I don't know..."

"I'm not asking you to do anything I would-
n't do for you."

"Yeah? Then where's my ticket to the PD
barbeque as your date?" Clay fired back. He
breathed out while raking his fingers through
his hair. He should say no. He really, really
should say no.

But when had he last been able to deny Seth
a single thing he wanted?

"Fine," Clay relented. "For one drink. One.
Then we go back home. I hardly ever have the
night off, and I want to enjoy myself."

"You couldn't do that in a bar?"

"While guarding your ass?" When Seth blinked, Clay burst into laughter. "You don't get it, do you?" he managed. "Oh, God, are you in for a surprise." He tapped the small microphone on his desk. "Jeri, we're good to go. Send in the fresh meat."

"I don't get what?" Seth asked as the door gave a discreet buzz and clicked open. Clay made shushing gestures with his hands as a man, big enough to play university fullback, edged in. He held a sheet of paper twisted into a fan in his massive hands. He was dark as melted chocolate with muscles upon muscles, and a shy if brilliant smile.

Clay's heart gave a small flutter. *Oh, yeah. Daddy like.*

"Hi," he said casually. "Come on in. I'm Clay."

"Hello. Richard," the giant said in a deep, burly voice that sent shivers up and down Clay's spine. "Pleased to meet you."

"Will those chairs fit him?" Seth blurted. A quick glance at him and he appeared to be dazed by Richard's sheer size. He'd taken on his 'cop' stance, arms loose and ready to swing.

Richard gave Seth a curious look as he sat down in one of the chairs. The wood creaked a little, but seemed otherwise okay. "Who's your… er… friend?"

"Bodyguard," Seth rapped out. "PD."

"Seth!" Clay yelped.

"Just here to make sure you're on the level."

Richard's eyes widened a bit. He gave Clay another uncertain look. "Hey, I thought this place was up-and-up. Is your man there doing some kind of sting?"

"No," Clay answered honestly, "he's just a pain in the ass. Let's get comfortable, Richard. Do you have a nickname?"

"Just Richard." The big man was looking more and more uncomfortable. "Look, is my name going to go down on some kind of sheet for being gay?"

"It's not a crime," Seth said flatly. "Okay, in some states it is. But that's not what I'm here for."

"Why is he here?"

"To be a pain in *my* ass?" Clay offered. "Richard, don't freak out, okay? Seth, why don't you step outside?"

"Staying right here, thanks."

Richard shook his head. "I'm starting to think this was a bad idea."

No, no! Stay right here. You and all your muscles. A man like this was a tasty dish, the kind Clay had ached to taste for years. Someone like that in his life would do the trick of getting Seth right out of his mind and back into the status of platonic housemate, right where he belonged.

"Everything's cool," Clay attempted to reassure Richard. "No worries. Hey, you want a drink?" He indicated a small mini-fridge by the side of the table. "I think they have cola, root beer, mineral water --"

"I think I should go." Richard made as if to stand up.

Nooo! Clay reached out with one hand. "Calm down, man."

"Easy for you to say," Richard fired back. "Look, either I'm being played or this is some kind of undercover operation. I can't afford either of those. I'm gone."

With the vision of muscles retreating into the distance, Clay finally blurted out the question: "But why?"

Richard stood, sighed, ran a hand across the top of his head, and said in a low voice: "I'm not out yet. Not even to my wife."

Clay's jaw dropped.

Behind him, Seth burst into laughter.

Oh, yeah. I can tell this speed dating thing is going to go just *great.*

* * *

From where he sat hunched over the bar, Clay couldn't see anything of what was going on around him. He'd already tossed back one shot and while that fermented in his belly, he waited listlessly for the bartender to take notice of the poor schmuck in need of a refill.

A full glass of bourbon slid into viewing range. Clay reached out and snagged the thing, sitting up to chug it down. As he did so, he caught sight of Seth standing behind him, a matching glass in hand. "Cheers," he said with a huge grin.

Clay put down his glass.

"Aw, now come on. What kind of attitude is that? I bought you a drink." Seth slid into the empty bar stool at Clay's side. "I got rid of the Closeted Cheater. The way I figure it, you owe me a toast."

"You want toast? Go to a diner. Leave me alone." Clay pushed the bourbon away and sank back down into his depressed slump. After a moment, Seth's still-full glass joined his.

Silence fell between them like a thick blanket. Seth fidgeted with the bar top, tapping his fingers in a rhythm, then raising up in his seat to read the labels on the bottles in front of them. Clay stayed put, hands over his eyes.

"Need a refill?"

"Yes, please," Clay muttered. His empty disappeared.

"Same again?"

"God, yes."

"You don't want the one your friend bought for you?"

"Fuck, no."

"Your loss. That's the good stuff." The bartender turned away, selected one bottle from the massed ranks, and poured a fresh shot. Handing over the new drink, he patted Clay on the shoulder. "Look, darling. I suggest you get it together toot sweet, understand me? Otherwise you're going to lose your friend there to the sharks."

Clay parted his fingers to peer at the bartender, a thin, tall man with short brown hair. Pretty damn cute, he had to admit. "There are sharks out tonight?" he asked, surprised.

"Circling. Mostly around your squeeze there, who is a prime cut of fresh new meat."

"Seth," Clay said to the man, who, to his credit, hadn't butted in yet. "You're being cruised. Use extra caution."

"Cruised?" Seth ran a finger around the rim of his shot glass. "What's crui -- oh, I remember. From one of your magazines." He fell silent for a beat. Clay heard the other shoe drop. "Oh, shit. They're cruising me?"

Clay opened his eyes wide enough to take a look at the mirror behind the bar. Yup, just as reported. Men in sharp suits and men in track clothes were all finding an excuse to ever-so-casually walk past and ogle Seth in his workout gear. Soft T-shirt and short shorts that exposed way too much lean tanned muscle for Clay's own comfort.

"Yup," he said. "They're cruising you." *Good taste, those guys. Bad manners, though. They are treating him like a prime cut, not a person. And okay, I've been plenty guilty of that in the past, but he's not just any guy. He's Seth. A good man, a great cop, and nobody's boy-toy.*

At least I can be reasonably sure he's coming home with me.

"Hey!" Seth jumped. "Someone just pinched my ass!"

"Probably the brunet in the vest," Clay observed in a monotone. "I've seen him before. He likes to do that."

"God, if I tried pinching a woman's ass at random like he just did, she'd knock me out." Seth stared at the retreating sneak-groper with amazement. "Does this go on all the time?"

"Hmm." Clay lifted his glass and swirled the dark amber liquid inside. "How many guys have offered to buy you a beer?"

"Maybe five or six -- hey, wait a second."

"Now that, I'll drink to." Clay lifted the shot to his mouth and tipped it back. The cool smoothness and harsh bite hit him at once like pure nectar from the gods and a kick in the pants from Satan. "You, my friend, are being given the royal treatment."

"You're kidding."

"Not a bit." With the atmosphere between them relaxing a little, Clay sat up and tried to explain to Seth. "Look, here's how it works. You've read my magazines, fine. But you of all people should know that practice is a completely different thing from theory. Take for example, Mr. Business Suit coming in at ten o'clock."

"It's that late already?"

"No, you dope." Clay elbowed Seth. "Don't turn around to look at him. Just watch the mirror."

Seth obeyed. Clay divided his attention between housemate and approaching sleazeball, nodding to himself when the man performed exactly as expected. A slow, steady approach, his eyes fixed on Seth's shapely back. Slowing down as he came closer, a longer look, and then the pause.

"Now." Clay nodded. "Turn around and look at him. Just for a few seconds, but be careful to meet his eyes."

Seth frowned, but apparently his trust in Clay extended far enough to venture into the unknown. He swiveled on his bar stool, pure sex in motion, and locked gazes with the Suit. After a moment Suit grinned, nodded in the direction of the bathrooms, and casually ambled on in that direction.

Clay nodded and started chasing the last drops of his drink. "And that, my friend, is being cruised."

Seth frowned. "All I did was stare him down. Where's the sexy part come in?"

"Basically, you just agreed to have sex with him in the bathroom stalls." Clay caught Seth before he lunged up away from the bar. "Whoa, whoa, easy, tiger. Not good manners to start pummeling the innocent scum."

"He actually thought I was going to -- that I was interested in --"

"And then some. You held that look for a few seconds too long. In cruiser-speak, you invited him to board your decks and set sail on the sea of love." Clay slid his glass forward. "Refill?"

The bartender obliged. Seth hunkered down into Clay's previous position, gripping his forehead. "This isn't like a binding obligation, is it?" he whispered anxiously. "He's not going to come out here making a scene if I don't follow him?"

"*If* you don't?"

"Hell with that. *When* I don't." Seth shuddered. "So this is what it's all about. God, you hear so much about the nightlife at gay bars. I'd thought it'd be a lot more… I don't know… high class."

Clay dissolved into giggles, helped somewhat by the smooth slide of alcohol. "Seth, get a grip. We're talking about guys, here. The same kind of guys you hang out with on the force. They might happen to prefer ass to pussy, but they're still men. M, e, n. They're just as much of a pig to one another as the straight guys. And in places like this?" He shrugged. "Everything's pretty much just all about the sex. A gay bar is not somewhere you go to find suave and debonair types just waiting to politely ask you for a cuppa and some civilized conversation."

"Jesus." Seth slumped onto the bar. "Okay, lesson learned. I know about cruising now. No eye contact." He paused. "I can still look at you, right? That's allowed?"

"Yeah." Clay grinned at their reflections in the mirror. He noticed Seth looking up to meet his own gaze. "Have a drink. Everything's better with a smooth one blazing its trail of fire down into your gut."

"I hear that." Seth took a measured sip. "I guess I shouldn't have gone into this expecting some kind of bright new world, huh? All pretty and witty and --"

"Finish that sentence and I will be forced to strangle you."

"Whoa! Okay, I won't." Seth grinned and toyed with his glass. "It's just like the rest of the world, isn't it? I mean, you have a few surprises like Jeri -- and damn, it is true, men make the prettiest women -- but for the rest, it's all the same. Men being men, even men who are ladies."

"We're all pigs."

"Now there's a toast." Clay clinked glasses with Seth, who grinned and got down to the business of ordering himself a tall, cool draft from the bartender, who seemed more than amused to discover Seth was in fact straight. Listening to them talk, he let his own mind drift away.

So Seth had discovered there wasn't anything earth-shattering about being gay. No matter what a person's sexual preference, they were all pretty much the same underneath the skin. Good guys, bad guys, sleazy lowlifes and nice types.

"Hey, Seth," he said abruptly. "Does this change what you think about me?"

Seth quirked an eyebrow. "No," he said simply. "Why would it? I'm a pretty bright bulb, Clay. I look at you and see the same guy I share a house with. The guy I've always known. Doesn't matter what you like in bed. I just know you're someone I get along with, like a lot, and enjoy spending my time with."

Yeah. But I bet Jeri would have had a better chance at winning your heart, at least until the clothes came off. Clay glumly took another sip. He assessed his level of drunkenness, and judged himself to be just far enough off the scales to blurt out what he'd been thinking all night:

"You're the best looking guy in here, Seth. You realize that? And I'm the one who gets to go home with you."

Silence. Clay felt Seth turn to stare at him, but refused to buckle under the weight of the gaze. He waited it out. One… two… three… four…

"No kidding?" Clay exhaled a breath he didn't realize he'd been holding. Seth's voice held honest surprise and gratitude. "That's big of you, man. Thanks."

Then, Seth nudged their elbows. "You're not that bad yourself," he mumbled, before diving into his beer.

Clay let himself grin broadly. He raised his glass. "To a beautiful friendship," he said proudly before doing the shot.

Seth laughed. "You're tanked off your ass."

"Oh, shut up."

And kiss me.

Yeah, right.

Chapter Five

"Okay, big guy. We're getting out of the car now." Seth leaned over to give Clay a light push. His friend gazed back at him through bleary eyes, nodded, smiled goofily, and slumped against the passenger door.

"Out is good," Clay said, not making a single move to get there. "No more moving streets. Nuh-uh, the car was still. I felt it be still. The streets run. Run right past you." He waved with five fingers, tracking their movement. "Still waters run deep."

"Pretty damn philosophical for a guy in your condition." Seth relaxed in his seat and grinned at Clay. He'd known the man couldn't hold his liquor, but then he'd gone and mixed it with beer straight from the tap. Good thing he'd given Seth lessons on gay bar etiquette before then, or they might have been in real trouble.

It'd taken some finesse, for example, to convince everyone that he and Clay were better off being left alone. Damn, there had been a bunch of really horny guys in the smoky little dive they'd holed up at.

Seth shook his head in wonder, remembering just how many offers he'd turned down. He suddenly understood women a whole lot better. Funny, really. He'd always thought he'd love to be the hot topic everyone wanted a piece of, but after a while he'd felt like -- meat. How did Clay cope with it every time he wanted a quiet drink?

Maybe that'd be why Clay hadn't gone out much in the past few months.

"You feel like heading inside?" Seth asked casually, catching Clay's wavering hand in his own and bringing it down to rest on Clay's knee. "Get into your nice cool bed, grab a glass or two of water, maybe some aspirin?"

One baleful eye zeroed in. "I am not drunk," Clay enunciated. "I know what I'm doing."

"Easy, easy. Just offering suggestions."

Clay had gone stiff with injured pride. "I think I can handle it by myself," he said, far too distinctly and carefully for true sobriety. "Just tell me where the door handle is, and I'll…" His voice trailed off. "Do something. Don't know what yet, but I will. You just watch."

"Bet you will," Seth soothed. "How about this? You let me give you a hand."

Clay started giggling. "If only you would," he spluttered after a minute. "You really don't have any idea, do you?"

Seth frowned, then filed that question away for later examination. "I'm offering one now," he said carefully. "Sit up straight, okay? I'm going to come around to your side and help you out."

"All right. If you can't have cake, a cookie's good enough." Clay giggled some more, arranging himself in what he probably imagined to be a ramrod position. "Help me out, can't you help me," he sang. "Somebody help me."

"On my way." Seth shook his head, amused, as he undid his own seatbelt and scooted out. Clay made one hell of a cute drunk. Rumpled and disheveled as he'd gotten, but still so good-natured, he made Seth think of a puppy again. A little spaniel who'd gotten into a dish of beer. Still ready to play, but weaving on its paws.

He chuckled as he crossed the front of the car, taking peeks through the windshield to make sure Clay hadn't collapsed. Nope; he still sat upright, and even saluted once when he caught Seth sneaking a look. Seth could hear his muffled laughter, and couldn't hold back his own grin. That was his buddy, all right.

One arm was ready to catch Clay in case he fell when Seth opened the passenger door. Clay cocked his head at the apparition, then, with solemn pomposity, shook Seth's hand.

"You are so very tanked," Seth informed Clay, leaning over him to unclick the seatbelt. "You're lucky I stopped at two and we stayed there long enough for me to sober up. A bar that serves coffee -- not a bad idea. Have you and Anthony been there together?"

"Toni?" Clay smiled beatifically. "My sweetie."

"Is he, really?"

"We've been there. To that place. Oh, yeah. They love Antonyeye. Call him their little boy and then laugh when he smacks 'em for it. He can drink me under the table any night of the week. Uh-huh." Decisive nod. "Then he calls a cab and the next day I have to figure out where the hell I left my car."

"That's Anthony." Seth slid an arm around Clay's shoulders. He breathed in, smelling the faint scent of Clay's soap and the rich spice of the cologne he'd slapped on earlier in the evening, along with rich Kentucky bourbon and microbrew.

Didn't make for a bad combination. Better than some of Sophie's French perfumes, for sure. He hadn't known whether to murmur in appreciation or politely ask what had just died.

"Hey." Clay focused on Seth. "You've got your arm around me." Up came the sunny smile. "That's nice. You look real good right there. You do. You look… good. So good."

"I do what, buddy?" Seth asked before the words processed their way through to his brain. Startled, he turned to look down at Clay. Clay, who sat completely at his ease, snuggling into the crook of Seth's arm.

"You look good on me," Clay explained earnestly. "You gotta know I've dreamed… thought about… but there was Sophie, and no way, right? But here you are, and here am I, and…" The hand began waving again. "It's all good, yeah? Everything's okay now."

"Sure thing." Seth could hear the absent tone in his own voice. Clearing his throat, he tugged at Clay. "Can you stand up?"

"Rather stay right here." Clay tugged back. "You ever sat in the front seat of a car with someone, Seth? Really just sat with 'em and said, 'this is nice'? All the way home, I kept thinking it over and over again. You're great to be with." The smile turned sweet -- gentle. "You gotta know you're a prize."

"Oh, yeah, the booby prize," Seth joked to cover his confusion, and his discomfort with things that were rapidly becoming clear. "Up, up, and away. Out of the car, Clay. Come on, now."

Grumbling, Clay allowed himself to be pulled along. When he stood on his own two feet, Seth's arm still supporting him, he weaved to and fro and blinked in rapid succession. "When did the trees learn how to dance?"

Seth stifled a snort of laughter. "Last night."

"The waltz?"

"Nope. Fox-trot."

"Who taught them?"

"That'd be me. Tomorrow we're gonna work on the tango. But first, we get you inside to bed. Sound like a plan?"

"Bed. Mmm." Clay leaned against Seth. "I think," he said after a fragrant pause that made Seth's head start to spin, "I need a little help."

"Right here for you."

"Only a little bit." Clay attempted to gauge the distance between finger and thumb, ending up with a snap. "Hey! Did you see what I just did?"

"Maestro. You can play the music for the trees."

"Dancing trees," Clay snickered, tucking his head into Seth's shoulder. "Can I have one in my bedroom?"

"Oh, yeah. A little bonsai. We'll show it how to flamenco."

"Cool." Clay rocked slightly back and forth. "Cool."

"We're all good." Seth gently pushed Clay back upright and helped steady him on his feet. Then, with a careful nudge, he eased them forward. "One step at a time, that's the way. Come on, hang with me. We'll get you safe inside."

Slowly, they wove a path up to their door. Clay blinked owlishly and fumbled at a pocket. "Keys," he said in explanation. "Gotta have some of those."

"You're in luck. I happen to have some of my very own."

"No kidding?" Another blink. "How'd you do that? Make a copy when I was getting another... thing I was drinking. They have a machine in the bar?"

"Clay, pal, I live here, too."

"Oh." Clay considered the statement with weighty gravity. "Right, yeah. Sorry. I forgot. I thought it was just me and Toni."

"Anthony's never lived with you, goofball."

"Shows what you know." Clay elbowed Seth. "We did. Shared a place when he first got out of college. Was looking for his... his own... space, thass it." Clay laughed, full and free. "He had all these glittery things, and I had my beanbag. Good old beanbag. Thought he'd claw my face off when I left a cold pizza on the floor."

"No kidding?" Seth had no idea if this fantasy was the result of a liquor-addled brain, or if Clay were on the level. One thing for sure, Clay did make an entertaining as well as an easygoing drunk. "What happened then? Here, hold on to me while I get my keys out."

Clay happily slid his arms around Seth's waist. "He made me eat it," he said solemnly, but with a huge grin. "After he'd stepped in it getting out of bed."

Seth couldn't help himself -- he cracked up. "If we're talking about the same Anthony, I believe you."

"Oh, yeah. Toni, Toni, Tone. My Toni." Clay sniffled. "Bestest friend ever. Except you. I like you. A whole lot."

"Bet you do. I'm irresistible, right?" Seth waited for the answer, wondering if Clay were drunk enough to answer honestly.

"You so are," Clay responded easily, tucking his head back into Seth's shoulder. Seth found himself on the receiving end of a warm hug. "You're just about one hundred and ten percent perfect."

Seth's hands closed on cool metal. "That a fact?"

"No doubt." Seth stiffened as he felt warm lips on his neck. "And you're coming home with me. I'm the luckiest guy there ever was."

"Just giving you a little help when you need it, Clay."

"Nice guy," Clay mumbled. He watched as Seth slid the key into their lock. "Look at that," he marveled. Then, he swayed again, turning slightly pale. "I think maybe I need to sit down."

"Not yet, big guy," Seth said, nudging the door open with one hip. "We're close, but no cigar so far. You're going straight to bed."

"Bed," Clay agreed, starting to smile again. "Tuck me in?"

"Sure thing," Seth agreed. "Let's just get you there first, okay?"

Clay nodded, and somehow Seth managed to get them through the doorway together. Not far to Clay's room -- everything opened off the hallway from the kitchen. A few tricky bits of navigation were involved, such as getting around the kitchen table, through another doorway, and Clay's insistence on stopping to examine one of Anthony's paintings that hung in the hallway.

"It's beautiful," he decided, after describing how the brush strokes went up and down, in and around, and swirled from side to side. "Just like Anthony. Wish I was..." He swallowed. "Wish I was what he needed. But maybe he'll find someone. Like I found you."

"You were lucky," Seth found himself saying. Then, his throat closed up, and he couldn't find another single word. Luckily, he didn't have to. They were through the door to Clay's bedroom.

Seth fumbled after a light switch for a few seconds before deciding they didn't need it. He knew this room as well as his own, and he could find Clay's bed in the dark.

A few more steps and they were at ground zero. Seth carefully angled Clay at the optimum position in relation to the bed, calculating angle and trajectory around the likelihood of flopping limbs, then let go. With a happy whoop, Clay fell -- as Seth had hoped, on his bed, if at a slightly diagonal slant.

"That was fun!" he enthused as Seth lifted his feet and slid them into place. "Let's do it again! You try, too."

Seth paused to put a hand on Clay's forehead. "Sorry, hon. I don't think you'd respect me in the morning."

"Hon." Clay, damn him, seized on the teasing word and turned it into something else. A softly breathed endearment. "You're sweet, too. Taking such good care of me."

As Seth watched, oddly unable to move, Clay reached up and took Seth's hand in his own. He pulled the appendage down and pressed a kiss to Seth's palm, then closed his fingers around the warmth left by his lips.

"A really good guy," Clay whispered before his eyes fluttered shut.

Seth felt about two inches tall. Damned if he could open his hand, either. "Clay?" He pushed the man with his knee. "You awake?"

Deep, even breathing answered him.

Okay, fair enough. Seth reluctantly pried Clay's fingers away from his own and eased the man's arm down on top of his blanket. Quilt? Looked new, whatever it might happen to be. He wouldn't want to ruin that with the inevitable result of getting tanked. Seth pondered the problem, then stood up and went back out into their hallway, heading for the kitchen.

When he returned, it was with an old sheet, torn in half, a glass of water and two painkillers. The water and pills went on Clay's bedside table, where he'd be sure to see them when he woke, and the soft old sheets on either side of his head to protect the quilt in case anything got spilled.

The job done, Seth stood up to study Clay. The guy didn't earn a fortune at the radio station, and his clothes were in a sorry state. They'd be even worse if he slept in them overnight and then had a bad morning after.

He should probably take them off.

Half of Seth quailed at the thought with a hearty, heterosexual *oh, no way* -- but the other part, quivering with curiosity, couldn't stop poking its nose in. "Clay?" he whispered. "Clay, man, I'm going to get you a little more comfortable, all right? Not trying to do anything wrong here. Just helping you out."

Clay stirred and murmured. His mouth curved into a soft smile. Watching him, Seth felt his heart contract with a mix of sorrow and something he couldn't put a name to. "Just don't be mad at me tomorrow morning," he said softly, touching Clay's forehead again. He couldn't have explained why he did. It just felt right.

Pulling away felt wrong.

Shaking his head at himself, Seth started with the hoodie. It unzipped down the front, the metal sounding loud in the hush of Clay's room. Seth winced, but Clay didn't flinch. "Arms first," Seth said soothingly. He lifted one, limp and unresponsive, and threaded it out of a hoodie sleeve. An arm underneath Clay's shoulders and he was able to tug the garment off via the second sleeve. Seth tossed it on the floor, mentally noting the need to take

it to the washing machine as soon as he finished.

Clay shifted in his sleep, still smiling.
"Good dreams?" Seth asked quietly, grinning
back at his friend. "Thinking about that cute
redhead at the agency? Man, I've seen trannies
in my day, but never anyone who pulled it off
like she did. Can't believe I missed the signs.
Jeri, was it? Oh, yeah." He smoothed his hand
down Clay's chest without thinking -- then
froze.

What the hell was he doing? Male chest,
flat and hard, with no soft swell of breasts or
dip and curve of belly. Nothing but lean muscle and the beginnings of a six-pack. "Hey,"
Seth said, knowing he sounded like an idiot,
"you really have been working out. Good job,
man."

He fell silent. Any minute now, he'd be
moving his hand. Any old minute.

His fingers disobeyed the mental impera-
tive. Slowly, they unfolded, fanning across
Clay's breastbone, broad enough to reach almost from nipple to nipple. Seth found himself
studying them in fascination. He'd seen Clay
with his shirt off before. Washing cars, watching TV, stepping out of the shower.

Never had wanted to touch the skin, though.
Never felt the urge to scratch lightly at the soft
flesh. Was it the soap? Or was this just Clay in
the raw? He could feel Clay's heart beating

with a slow, steady rhythm, and had the craziest urge to lay his head down and listen.

Seth gave a small shudder. His emotions were playing around like he'd never felt. Confusion, curiosity, puzzlement, and… desire? He swallowed hard as he recognized the sensation. Couldn't be. He was straight. Always had been, always would be.

Right?

Had to be. Which didn't explain a thing about why he was climbing up on the other side of the bed, toeing his sneakers off onto the carpet, and stretching out beside Clay.

I'm just keeping an eye on him, Seth thought. *Making sure he's okay. That's what friends are for, right?*

"You get some sleep," he said, not reaching out for Clay, no matter how much he wanted to. He didn't understand himself yet, and he didn't need to get Clay tangled up in yet another of his own messes. "I'll be right here if you need anything, okay?"

Clay breathed in and out, steady and deep.

Seth nodded, the pillowcase soft and cool underneath his cheek. "Thought so," he whispered, and let himself fall silent, still, and unmoving.

Like a guardian statue, he watched over his friend, making sure nothing happened.

He'd keep his eyes open all night if he needed to.

* * *

Bong. Bong. Bong.

Three A.M., and Seth still hadn't been able to fall asleep. Pretty hard to, with his mind whizzing around in a dozen different directions on flights of fancy he couldn't hope to keep up with. He'd chase after one, and another would distract him into following.

He'd given up on lying down thirty minutes in. The temptation to reach out and touch was too much. There'd been an almost magnetic pull, as if his arm demanded its rightful place stretched over Clay's chest. And that -- no. Just, no. Seth couldn't cope, so he'd strategically retreated.

Sitting up with his back braced against the headboard, a pillow across his lap, Seth watched Clay sleep. Again, not anything new. He'd seen Clay snoozing on the sofa during early mornings when he'd been too tired after the all-night shift to make it to his bedroom. Even tossed a throw blanket over the guy and ruffled up his hair, laughing when Clay made small irritated noises and twitched away from him.

What would Clay do now, if Seth gave in to the need rising within him, reached out, and carded his fingers through the soft black tumble spread across Clay's pillow? His fingers twitched, reminding him of Clay's tender kiss. The center of his palm felt warm, as if he held a live coal.

And if he had an ember in his hand, it didn't hold a candle to the fire alight in his belly. Shaking his head, not understanding in the least, Seth edged a little further away from Clay. "Sorry, man," he whispered. "This is all just a little much for me, you know?"

Clay murmured something in his sleep and turned slightly, tilting his face toward Seth. Seth stared at it, tracing the lines and angles as if he were seeing them for the first time. This didn't make sense. None of it did.

If he'd been in bed with a woman, what would he have been doing? More than likely he wouldn't be hunched up like a spider. No, he'd be down by her side, keeping her warm, spooned up against him. Sleeping lightly, waiting for the morning to break so he could help her to the aspirin and water.

Clay, though, definitely not a woman. A man, and his housemate. The guy he loved like a brother. *A brother,* Seth insisted to his unquiet mind. *Nothing more.*

Why, then, did his eyes keep straying to the long lines of Clay's body spread out on the quilt? Every line of the man held a strange sort of fascination for him. The curve of an arm pulled up against his side, the broad expanse of chest, the ridges on his belly, and the square jut of his chin, thrust up as he dreamed of things Seth couldn't begin to comprehend.

What was it like to *really* be gay? Seth shook his head. God, he'd been a fool. Starting this whole game off as a way to annoy Sophie into leaving, then getting interested in how the different world worked. Clay must have been so pissed at Seth treating his lifestyle like one big amusement park ready and waiting for him to come play. He'd disrespected the man, and what had he gotten in return?

Understanding. Jokes. The same warm acceptance Clay exuded for everyone who came close enough to touch. He hadn't treated Seth like a social moron or a rude bastard, no. He'd let Seth in, and showed him the ropes.

Seth shook his head. He wouldn't have been so understanding, himself, if Clay had asked him about being straight. More than likely, he'd have pointed the guy in Anthony's direction and told him to have at it. In fact, hadn't he been thinking about the same thing in the shower? Seth winced as he remembered the thought.

And fuck, could he get any more insensitive than jerking off while thinking about warm brown eyes that had only ever been friendly to him? Granted, the whole thing had taken him by surprise, too. He'd been wrong in how he handled the aftermath, though. Using Clay like a blow-up doll just to piss off his thankfully ex-girlfriend.

Clay deserved more than the shoddy treatment Seth had dealt out to him. He needed someone in his life who'd understand, who'd offer a shoulder when he needed one.

Slowly, Seth reached out and rested his hand on Clay's forearm. He felt so warm, so soft, and so good. Touching him gave Seth's stomach a turn, just like it was the seventh grade all over again and he was sneaking his first kiss underneath the bleachers during gym class.

What would life be like, really, if it had been a Joey instead of a Joanna who he'd kissed? Seth exhaled softly, realizing he really didn't know the answer to that question.

Would it be so bad, being attracted to a man? Seth gave in to temptation, just the tiniest bit, and let his eyes roam over the length of Clay's body again. He wasn't sure he got the whole lack of breasts thing, but if he were looking at Clay through different eyes, he could see the appeal.

All that smooth, flat skin just begged for a hand to caress up and down the dips and planes. Seth could see himself starting with one finger right between both nipples, drawing a line down over the muscles to the thin trail of hair that disappeared into his jeans, and…

He jerked his hand back before it ventured any further. God! He'd actually done it. Reached out and felt Clay up like a -- Seth felt sick. Disgusted with himself.

But for all that, his hand tingled. Stirring where he sat, Seth felt the beginning of an erection start between his legs. And Clay, well, he was already there. Good dreams? Seth would say so. But were they brought on by his touch?

Seth drew back, wrapping his arms around his knees. Old girlfriends and guys he'd hung out with in the past flashed in front of his eyes, each one of them offering some piece of advice: *run away, stay right where you are, touch him, don't touch him, wake him up, let him sleep, tell him everything in the morning,* and *don't you dare say a word.*

It didn't seem right leaving Clay all by himself, but Seth knew he couldn't stay any longer. Carefully rolling off the bed so as not to wake the man up, he rummaged around in the dark until he found a folded blanket. He opened it up and spread it over Clay's body, carefully smoothing down all the wrinkles.

"Sorry," he whispered. "I'm just confused, that's all. You understand, don't you, Clay?" He swallowed hard. "I think I know your secret now. Never get drunk around me again, understand? I'm not ready to deal with this yet."

One last touch on Clay's foot, and Seth turned to leave the room. "You don't want me, anyway," he said softly. "I'm not good enough for you, Clay. What you need is someone who can really be there for you. Me, I can't even make up my mind about a kiss on the hand."

He paused in the doorway, a thought occurring to him. "I'll make it up to you. The speed dating, the cruising. I'll take care of you. Help you find someone who could be way better than I could ever hope, even if I did know what to think about myself right now. I can't be what you want, not yet. I think you know as much. So… starting tomorrow, we're going to work on getting you someone good to bring home.

"And I'm going to work on forgetting this ever happened."

Chapter Six

Seth never did make it to sleep that night. He tried lying down, sure, but after an hour or two of turning from one side to the other, punching his pillow into shape and flipping it over to find a cool side, he gave up. Instead, he went to sit by his window and listened to the comforting sounds of surf pounding into sand. In and out they rushed, but for once in his life they failed to calm him down.

His head raced with thoughts he couldn't understand, much less break down into quantifiable components. Clay, with his kisses and his sweet words -- they defied logic. Seth couldn't wrap his head around why the man would have acted as if, well, he wanted Seth. In *that* way. Seth wasn't stupid; he knew all the signs. If Clay had been a woman, he still would have tucked her in and not taken advantage, but he'd have been all but jumping up and down with excitement at the *she likes me, she likes me* of the whole situation.

But this? With Clay? Seth shook his head. Dawn was rising outside his window. God, had he really stayed up all night long? He shook his head again, then closed his eyes and tried to picture the golden rays gleaming over the blue surface of the ocean. No luck. The only thing he kept coming back to was Clay's eyes, warm and brown. Trusting and… loving.

This called for drastic measures.

Pancakes.

And someone to share them with. A person who'd understand not only Seth's dilemma, but have the inside scoop on Clay as well. Seth could only think of one person who fit the bill. Anthony.

Quietly and carefully, watching out for any sudden, loud sounds that might wake Clay up next door, Seth picked up his phone and began to dial Anthony's number. *Ring. Ring.* He began to worry that he was already awake and in his studio, where he didn't have a phone. *Ring.* Then, he worried that Anthony was fast asleep and ignoring the phone. *Ring.*

His heart gave a huge thump of relief when he heard the other line pick up, along with some muffled cursing and the clunking noises of someone trying to balance a receiver between their ear and shoulder.

"This had better be good," Anthony said, sounding cranky. It'd take a brave man to face the tough little guy down like this, but Seth didn't see that he had any choice.

"Clay," he said, and waited for it.

"Clay?" Some of the fogginess cleared from Anthony's voice. "Is he all right? Where is he?"

"He's here, and he's fine. It's me."

More sounds, as if Anthony were sitting up in the tangle of his sheets and comforters. Seth could see him so clearly, folding his legs underneath himself and leaning his elbow on one knee. "What's wrong with you, hon?"

Seth sighed. "Everything?"

"And it's got to do with Clay?"

"Very much so."

"Right." Anthony made a clucking noise with his tongue. "Seaside Diner, thirty minutes? I'll be the one with messy hair because someone woke me up at the ass crack of dawn."

Relief rushed into Seth's stomach. "Thank you, Anthony. God, thank you."

"You're paying," Anthony informed him. "And now that I'm awake, I'm going to eat like a horse and to hell with the calories."

"Deal." Seth didn't care if he didn't have enough money after last night's bar crawl. He'd use plastic if he had to. "You have no idea how much I appreciate this."

"Feed me, and then we'll talk." Anthony snorted. "I'm so easy. A few eggs and strips of bacon, and I spill all my secrets."

"There are secrets to spill? And don't forget about pancakes."

"French crepes." Seth could hear Anthony's smirk. "I told you I wasn't going to go easy on this breakfast. Now get dressed up, tux and tails, mister, and get on over there. I'll be waiting for you."

"Bless you, Anthony." Seth hung up the phone and searched the room, scanning for something -- anything -- that didn't smell like Eau de Bar, or looked reasonably clean. Finally, he settled on a loose pair of sweatpants and a clean workout T-shirt. Not exactly fancy, but the Seaside Diner wasn't exactly haute cuisine, after all. A good shorefront greasy spoon that served up the best breakfast twenty-four seven that he knew of.

His favorite bolt-hole, aside from home, when he'd had a bad night. Anthony knew it, too. Good old Anthony.

Dressed, Seth opened his door with extra care and peered out through the hallway. Good; Clay's door was still firmly closed. He didn't want to risk waking the guy up. That way led to awkward conversations and decisions on whether or not to touch him as he'd always done, and Seth just wasn't ready to go there yet.

Tiptoeing out of the house, he locked the door behind him. Then he winced. His motorcycle, the good old chopper, would make enough noise to rouse the dead, much less one hungover man. He could take Clay's car, but that would leave Clay with no transport.

Nothing for it. Seth threw one leg over the saddle and let the bike coast down the driveway out into the street. Once there, he turned the key in the ignition and revved up her motor, speeding away fast as he could. He knew the way to the diner like the back of his hand, and he prayed that Anthony would have some answers for him.

If he didn't, Seth was screwed.

* * *

Clay sat up in his bed -- or tried to. A pounding head arrested him a few inches off the pillow. He slitted his eyes open and peered out at the world around him. *Oh, thank God.* Someone had left aspirin and a glass of water on his bedside table. With clumsy hands, he reached out and managed to fumble the pills into his palm. Popping them into his mouth, he grabbed the water next and sloshed it into his mouth. The pills went down, and he collapsed back onto his pillow.

What the hell had happened the night before? Last thing he remembered was taking shots at the bar Seth had dragged him to. Lots of shots. Groaning, Clay dry-washed his hand over his face. He put the water back in its place and used the second hand to rub his eyes. Jesus, this was the mother of all hangovers. There must have been more shots than he recalled.

How had he gotten home? Had to have been Seth. Clay struggled to recall the details, and slowly bits and pieces began to fade back into focus. Yeah… Seth had helped him to the car and buckled him in. There would probably have been a drive involved at some point.

The vague memory of dancing trees came back to him. Had he babbled about them? Clay groaned in embarrassment, burying his face further in the pillow. And then… and then…

Oh, shit. His eyes flew open. He'd kissed Seth. Just his palm, but all the same. More, he'd let his guard down. Treated Seth like a lover who was taking care of him after too much to drink.

Even though his head protested, Clay began to fumble his way out of bed. He realized he didn't have a shirt on as he went to straighten the hoodie he last remembered wearing, and his cheeks flushed red with embarrassment. Who'd taken it off? Him, or Seth? At least his pants were still on, thank God.

More memories floated into his mind. Seth had been so gentle, listening to all of Clay's yammering with good humor and then… Clay froze. Seth had lain next to him on the bed. He couldn't remember any touching, but the man had actually shared his bed and he couldn't recall anything beyond the fact!

Oh, man, if he'd only been sober. The devil rum, indeed. Clay stood, paused as the room swayed around him, then headed for the door. The knob proved a little hard to work as his hand was shaking, but eventually he wrestled the stubborn thing open. Stumbling out into the hallway, he steadied himself with a hand on the hallway wall, and peered around to find Seth's door.

Open.

"Hey, man," he mumbled, inching closer. "Look, I think we need to talk. About last night. You know."

He knocked. No response. "Look, I just want to apologize, okay? I don't remember what I did, but if I made you mad, then just --"

The door swung open. Clay stared inside. Seth's usually neatly-made bed was in disarray, and a chair had been pulled up to the window. His heart sank. He'd seen this kind of thing before, usually on nights when Sophie had been acting like a class-A bitch. Had Seth been so upset he hadn't been able to sleep, and then sat by the window until dawn? The sound that woke him must have been Seth's motorcycle revving up to leave.

Clay sagged against the doorframe. Seth, gone. No chance to talk things over and explain himself.

Well, hell.

* * *

Seth pushed open the door to the Seaside Diner. The waitress, a young girl with her head shaved almost to the scalp, greeted him with a grin. "Hey, man. Table for one?"

"Actually, no. I'm here with someone this morning." Seth scanned the booths. To his relief, he spotted Anthony's curly head in a booth, bent over a menu. Man, he could already feel the cash slipping out of his wallet. That little guy could flat eat. Seth didn't understand how Anthony managed to inhale such huge amounts of food and still keep his slender figure. Sophie never ate anything but steamed vegetables and on occasion, a tiny, carefully weighed portion of plain roasted chicken.

"That's my party over there," he said, pointing. "Hey, Anthony!"

"New squeeze, huh?" the waitress asked, grinning. "He's a hottie, man. Not the place I'd bring someone to impress him, but best of luck, yeah?"

Seth managed to grin. "He's not the one I'm interested in, but I'm hoping he can help me out with the one I do want." *I think. Maybe?* "Has he already ordered?"

"No, but he's drunk three iced teas and he's been making a list while he reads the menu." At Seth's dumbfounded expression, the hostess laughed and clapped him on the back. "Get over there before your friend decides to order one of everything."

Accepting a menu of his own, Seth tucked his motorcycle helmet under one arm and started to weave his way between booths. "Anthony!" he called when he was close enough not to disturb too many diners bent over their Big Skipper Specials. "Hey, Toni!"

His head came up, and that wide, Anthony smile broke across his lips. Felt like a warm, soothing balm. Seth basked for a moment before he joined the man, sliding into the booth across from him. He glanced down, realizing that Toni *had* made a list.

Anthony took the last sip of his tea and grinned at Seth. "So," he said without any pre-amble, "did the earth move for you?"

Seth spluttered. "Christ, Anthony!"

"Well? Did it, or not?"

"No! I wouldn't do that to Clay, not when he was drunk."

Anthony pounced. "But you wanted to, did-n't you?"

Seth realized his mistake a minute too late, and put his hand over his face. "You tricky lit-tle bitch," he mumbled. "You had that all planned out, didn't you?"

"Yes, and if you call me a bitch again, I'll empty this glass of ice on your lap," Anthony said sweetly. "Look, it didn't take a genius. A man like me sees a lot of things when it comes to his best friend, and that's my Clay. Hurt him, and I'll have your balls for a necklace."

"Anthony, back up!" Seth waved his hands in the air, forming a T sign. "Slow down. You're reading all kinds of things into the situation here that just don't apply. I don't even know if I... I mean, Anthony, I'm straight." He paused. "Aren't I?"

The look on Anthony's face changed from teasing to sympathetic. "Honey, you're the only one who can answer that question."

"That's a lot of help," Seth griped. "I don't understand myself, Toni, and I don't have a single clue as to what's going on. I mean, this all started out as a joke, right? A way to get Sophie off my back. But then we went drinking, and he had to be all nice and sweet and gentle, and oh, God, am I gay now?" He dropped his head onto the table with a thump.

"Are you, uh, ready to order?" Another waitress, one Seth didn't recognize through one barely open eye, stood in front of them, looking understandably nervous. "I can, you know, come back if you're not."

Poor kid looked like she wanted nothing more than to escape. Anthony jumped in with the save. "I think we need a few more minutes. Another tea for me, though."

The waitress nodded and beat feet. Anthony gave Seth's shoulder a thump. "Get with the program, buddy. You asked me out for breakfast, in your favorite stomping grounds no less, so I want to see you eat. No one ever accomplished anything good on an empty stomach."

"I don't know if I can." The thought of bacon and eggs had been unbelievably tempting before Seth had smelled them, but now he wasn't sure at all if he could keep a single thing down. "I'm tied up in knots inside, Toni, and you're worried about a pancake or two?"

"Pancakes, good idea!" The waitress came back with Anthony's iced tea. Anthony flashed her one of those wide smiles, and handed over the menu. "French crepes, two scrambled eggs, a side of bacon, and a side of seasoned red potatoes for me. Warm maple syrup for those crepes. For him, a small Fisherman's special. Butter on his pancakes."

Seth groaned.

The waitress took the menus hesitantly, then scribbled Anthony's request down on her notepad. "Be just a minute," she said. Then, after another second's pause, she offered: "If you are gay, it's not that bad. My best friend is gay, and he's a great guy."

As she fled, Anthony stared after her, shaking his head. "Girls these days," he said absently. "She can't be over eighteen, and she's already learning the ways of the fag hag. God bless America." He raised his fresh glass of tea in a toast. "Here's to the modern youth."

Seth sat up. "Anthony," he said, without patience for dancing it any longer. "What's going on with me? I've been straight all my life. Now, a couple of kisses with Clay and I'm starting to doubt myself."

"Hmm." Anthony stirred the ice in his glass with a straw. "Do you think it's all guys, or just him?"

"Say what, now?"

"Well, do you fantasize about Clay?"

"Anthony!"

"Come on, do you?" Anthony nudged a place mat towards him. "It's just Sister Toni here. All secrets spilled in confession remain confidential."

Seth sighed. "Yeah," he admitted grudgingly. "A couple of times."

"Such as when?"

"Once in the shower."

"Mmm. Bet you came like a pulse cannon."

Seth stared at Anthony accusingly. "That is so far off the list of things I want to discuss that it isn't even in the same ZIP code. There will be no discussion of my…" He fumbled.

"Ejaculatory competence?"

Seth closed his eyes tightly. "Yeah. That." When he opened up, Anthony was grinning at him like a cat who'd stolen the cream. "You're loving this, aren't you?"

Anthony shrugged. "I'm a yenta at heart. What can I say? More to the point, I'm not blind. I know how Clay looks at you."

"How does he look at me?" Seth's heartbeat sped up. He leaned forward, although he still wondered at himself and why he was doing so. He'd wanted Anthony to convince him he was straight -- hadn't he? "Like a friend, or…?"

"Honey, he wants you." Anthony took a long drink of tea. "He'd never say it himself, and he'd kill me if he knew I'd said a word about the matter, but you know as well as I do that Clay's had the hots for you since he moved in. He's just too much of a gentleman to say a word about it when he knows you don't swing that way." There came the grin again. "But now, looks like you might be starting to butter your bread on the other side."

Seth shook his head. "You're not being any help, you know. I came here for advice, and --" His mind backtracked. "Clay wants me?"

"Like a cigarette wants a match. Snap, crackle!" Anthony gestured with his hands. "The man has spent hour after hour keeping me awake with talk about how fantastic you are. Trust me, no gay man goes on and on and need I say, on, about a man unless he's interested." Another sip and a sly look. "Then there are the times he's just said it outright."

"Oh, man." Seth sat back. "Anthony, this is a whole lot to deal with. I could have handled pretending for a little while, but if Clay's really in love with me, and I -- I --" He faltered. "What if I love him back?"

Anthony pointed with his straw. "Love, or lust?" When Seth shook his head to stop him, he ignored Seth and plowed on. "There's a big difference, buddy. I know how you think. Sex equals good. Most of the time you lead with your small head. And in the interest of protecting my best friend, I have to ask the question." He leaned forward. "So?"

Seth took a deep breath. He sipped at the complimentary ice water to stall for time, but under Anthony's gimlet stare, felt his cushion melting away. "I don't know," he admitted at last. "I look at Clay, and I want to protect him. I want to do these strange things, like take him by the hand and just hold it."

"Do you want to kiss him? He's the kind of guy who could make you want to change your stripes."

Despite himself, a smile tugged at Seth's lips. "He is something else, isn't he? Back when I was interviewing for roommates, he stood out like a gem. Honest face, good hands, open attitude, and friendly. We clicked, you know? The gay thing didn't throw me for a second. We even joked about curfews and when someone could bring someone else home for the night."

"Love at first sight?" Anthony asked.

"No. Definitely not. But there was…" Seth frowned. "Something. An instant connection. I felt like I'd known him for years, and I'd only been around the guy for thirty minutes."

"And since then?"

Seth rolled his eyes. "God, Toni, you're in and out of our house all the time. Answer that question yourself."

Their food arrived, and Anthony made noises of appreciation at the crispy potatoes, fluffy eggs, chewy bacon, and massive plate of crepes with butter. Seth's own stomach grumbled in appreciation at the savory smell of his own two pancakes and one egg over easy. Picking up a fork, he dug in, taking a savory bite.

"You want him," Anthony said decidedly, taking a big bite of bacon. "A blind man could tell that much."

Seth choked on his egg. The waitress, hovering nearby to make sure everything was okay, looked at him in alarm. "Does he need the Heimlich maneuver?"

"Nah, he's fine." Anthony leaned over to thump Seth on the shoulder. "He's coughing, so there's oxygen getting through. Probably just what I said to him."

"Yeah," the waitress muttered, her eyes wide. "Don't ever spring that on a guy when his mouth's full."

"Depends on what it's full of, sweetie," Anthony said kindly. "I've got it from here. Go on and serve some other customers now, okay?"

The waitress scuttled away. When she was out of earshot, Seth leaned over and took Anthony's hand. "Come on," he begged. "Tell me what to do."

Anthony shook his head. "Only you can decide," he said, patting Seth's arm. "I can tell you this much: Clay cares about you, and you feel the same way. Sounds like the basis for a good relationship to me, no matter what orientation you might happen to be."

"Anthony…" Seth sighed. "I'm not good enough for him, okay? He needs someone who knows what they are. Someone who's comfortable with liking other men."

"You don't have to like other men. Just Clay." Anthony popped a chunk of potato into his mouth, chewed, and swallowed. He made a noise of appreciation. "I really have to start coming here more often. This is delicious."

"Anthony, leave the food alone. We're talking about serious stuff here."

"So am I. Breakfast is the most important meal of the day."

"Anthony!"

"Okay, okay." Anthony wiped his fingers on a napkin. He leaned forward, his face kinder than Seth had ever seen it. "All I'm saying is that maybe you do need more time to think about things. But you need to think about this, too: there's a tie between you. Maybe it's strong enough to bridge the gap between friends and lovers. Maybe not. But you don't get out of this by saying you're not good enough.

"I know you, too, Seth, and I know you're a good man. You give your whole heart to someone you love, and it hurts you like a bitch when things don't work out. Like Sophie. Don't tell me you don't have regrets about ending it with her, everything regardless."

Seth looked down, dejected. "I didn't treat her right," he mumbled. "I should have just been honest with her."

"In retrospect? Probably so. We were too caught up with the idea of the joke at the time to understand what it would do to her. But that's done, in the past, finito. Now, what you have to focus on is moving forward. You have to choose whether or not you want that to be alone, or with Clay."

Seth slumped in his seat. He picked at the edge of one crisp, golden-brown pancake. Giving him an arch look, Anthony went back to inhaling his eggs and bacon.

After a minute, Seth looked up. "Say that I do want to pursue this. What would Clay think?"

Anthony swallowed. "Truthfully? I think he'd feel like the luckiest man on Earth. I told you, he's wanted you since he moved in." He frowned. "Well, no. Wanting sounds like lusting, and that's not the point. What I'm trying to say is he's felt something for you. A thing that could go all the way, if you'd been willing."

"He's been carrying a torch all this time?"

"Flaming." Anthony lifted his glass of tea and tilted it at Seth. "So once again, I say: it's up to you, my friend. Take the time you need, but do make a decision."

The door jangled, and Anthony glanced up. "Uh-oh."

Seth stiffened. "Uh-oh? Uh-oh what, Anthony?"

"Your time just decreased by an infinite amount," he said, his face grim. "Don't look now, but Sophie just came in, and she looks like she's loaded for bear."

"Shit! How did she know I was here?"

"She's definitely looking for you. Oh, crap. She's spotted us. Don't look now -- I said, don't look now! Seth, you goon!"

He'd turned around to peer at the woman in question. He felt his face pale. "Toni, who is that with her?"

Anthony popped another bite of something into his mouth. "Judging from the suit, tie, and Bible under his arm, I'd say a minister. How she found one around here is anyone's guess."

"Oh, shit." Seth sat down, shaken. "She's tracked me down to make me marry her."

"It might not be that bad." Anthony raised up a little. "Then again, she is wearing white."

Seth's stomach twisted up in knots. "Do they see me?"

"Oh, yeah. And they're headed this way." Anthony looked at Seth with extreme serious-ness. "Time to choose, Seth. What do you feel for Clay? Enough to tell Sophie off a second time, or are you going to back down?"

Seth swallowed hard. He searched for words, but none were forthcoming. He felt himself begin to tremble. God, a man shouldn't have to answer questions like Anthony's right off the bat.

But what else could he do? What other choice did he have?

"There you are," Sophie said, her voice vi-cious, as she pulled up to the edge of the table. "I knew I'd find you here when I didn't see your bike at the house. Where else do you go when you have something on your mind?"

Seth made himself look her in the eye. She was beautiful as ever, but twice as cold. Her eyes almost snapped with ice as she glared at him. "Seth? Have you changed your mind about this whole 'gay' thing yet?"

Seth's mouth opened to answer her question, while his brain was still stalled in neutral, and said…

Chapter Seven

Clay lay alone in his bed, one arm flung out to the side where Seth would have lain the night before. His fingers idly stroked the sheets, as if he could pick up some residual warmth. A hair or a fiber. Something tangible, beyond his memories, to prove that Seth had stayed with him the night before.

Heaving a sigh, he brought his hand back up to his chest. What kind of fool was he, anyway? If Seth had hung around, it wouldn't have been out of any kind of romantic motivation. He'd just wanted to make sure his buddy was okay.

His buddy. Clay laughed softly, bitterly, since no one was around to hear. He'd admit it to himself -- he was so gone on Seth. Heart, soul, lock, stock, and barrel. He didn't want just friendship from Seth. He wanted love as well. Wasn't it his luck to have set his sights on a straight man?

Clay extended one leg and waggled his toes. He half-closed his eyes and let himself drift into a dream of how it could have been, how he'd have liked it to be…

"Hey, good morning." Seth elbowed the bedroom door open. He carried two plates,

one in either hand. "Gotta go back for the coffee, but there was no reason to let all this get cold."

"Breakfast in bed? Isn't that a little girly?" Clay joked.

Seth blushed. "Yeah, well, I have a sentimental side. Don't ride me too hard about it."

"How about I ride something else?" Clay sat up, accepting the plate and then putting it on his nightstand. He reached for Seth's hand, trapping it between both of his own, and tugging. Laughing, Seth only just managed to deposit his own breakfast on a flat surface before Clay managed to pull him down onto the bed -- and more importantly, onto Clay.

The two men looked at each other, eye to eye, from a distance of inches. "Morning," Seth whispered. Clay could feel the tickle of warm breath on his face. Could almost taste Seth's lips on his own. "How'd you sleep?"

"Like I was a kid again, without a single worry in the world."

"Mmm." Seth dipped down to kiss Clay as lightly as a butterfly's wing. Not nearly hard enough or long enough. "And how do you feel now that you're awake?"

"Like I can do anything, long as you're by my side. In my bed." Clay shifted, bringing his morning erection up into contact with Seth's groin. He felt a matching hardness there, and began to grin. "I know what you woke up feeling like," he teased.

Seth half-closed his eyes. "Oh, God, you're gonna kill me."

"Do you want me to stop?"

"Never." Seth rotated his hips slowly, grinding into Clay with a touch that was almost enough to bring them off. "I want you to lie right where you are. Don't move a muscle."

"Not even one muscle?" Clay brought one leg up to hook his foot around Seth's calf. "How about that one?"

Seth groaned as his erection in its loose sleep shorts slipped down between Clay's thighs. "I'll give you one freebie."

"Only one?" Clay brought his other leg around to Seth's upper leg, hugging him tight. "What about if I push my luck, like this?"

"You might push it all the way to very lucky," Seth breathed before kissing Clay again. A good kiss, just right for two men -- rough, bruising, and as filled with passion as a plum was with juice. Seth broke away to murmur as Clay began to rock, setting up a rhythm and friction between them. "Oh, yeah. Just like that. Keep doing it for me."

"Always," Clay whispered. "Always..."

Clay blinked, coming out of his daydream. A small beeping had woken him. Not his alarm clock, so what…? He frowned, flailing around on his bedside table until he found a small timer. "Why did I have this here?" he muttered to himself, turning it around and around. Then --

"Oh, shit!" The speed dating service! He'd set the timer as a back-up precaution against sleeping in too late. Usually, he'd turn off his alarm and roll right back over.

Not this morning, though. Today he had to be up and moving if he was going to get there in time. "Jeans, jeans, where are jeans?" he chanted as he shucked out of last night's clothes and dove into his closet, hunting for a fresh pair. It took some serious digging, but at last he unearthed a soft, worn pair from underneath a stack of T-shirts that had been loved and worn not wisely but too well.

He held one of them up to the light for a moment before spotting a hole right through the Myrtle Beach logo and discarding the thing.

Another hoodie? Nah, too warm. He could already feel the day heating up, and it might not be a scorcher but he'd sweat to death in terrycloth. Definitely tee weather. Catching up a simple white one, no emblem, he paired it with a loose, light blue overshirt. There, layers. Who said he couldn't be preppy?

Halfway through his rushing to get dressed, however, Clay screeched to a stop. He groaned and thumped himself on the forehead. Ten minutes ago, he'd been lying in bed dreaming of his one true love, and now he was running around like a crazy person trying to get ready to meet some fresh cattle on the hoof? Shouldn't he have paused for some kind of reflection, a sad goodbye to his dreams, or at least a promise to the dreamed-up Seth that he'd never lose his place as number one?

Clay slowly shook his head. He had to face up to the fact that no matter what he wanted, Seth was straight. He himself was not. Never the twain would meet, pranks and initiation rites notwithstanding. He couldn't lie around and mope over Seth like he had been for the past however many months.

Time to get out there, find that horse, and ride its cowboy off into the sunset.

No matter what his traitor heart had to say about it.

Clay shook his head again, pulling the shirt on. A little wrinkled, but it'd do. A quick trip to the bathroom to clean his teeth, swish with something astringently minty, and tousle his hands through his hair. He still smelled like a smoky bar, but he splashed on a little cologne (the kind Seth liked, his mind whispered to him) and decided it'd be good enough.

Out to his car, then, after finding his keys on the kitchen table desk with a post-it note labeled: HEY, CLAY. NEED THESE? Grinning, he snatched them up and headed for his beat-up old clunker. He even managed to whistle a tune as he went, something that probably didn't belong to any actual song, but sounded pretty good to him.

He loved Seth. Always would love Seth. But he couldn't wait around forever. Clay started up the car and put it in reverse, looking out the rearview mirror, backing away from his own personal Heartbreak Hotel and on to bigger, better things.

* * *

Clay slid into his seat behind the desk, running a hand through his hair and offering a sheepish grin. "Hey, uh, Michael. Sorry I'm late. The roads are just packed; well, you know what traffic is like with the tourist season just starting, and I should just shut up now and let you introduce yourself, shouldn't I?"

Michael, or so his name tag announced, stared at Clay through two kohl-ringed eyes. His black hair stuck up in spikes, and he had more piercings than Clay could count. Definitely two through each eyebrow, a bead on his nose, one on his chin, two through either cheek, but when it came to a tally on the earlobes, Clay gave up.

There were some definite points of interest to Michael. For one, the collar he wore. If Clay wasn't mistaken, it had originally been intended for a dog and adapted to one of the less selective S & M sets. Michael ran a finger under it as he stared at Clay, his mouth quirking up into a half-grin. Not exactly a friendly look on old Mikey, either.

Clay swallowed and tried to look away, but no luck. Michael sort of sucked everyone's line of sight to him, like some kind of black hole that demanded attention instead of matter. To give him credit, he earned it. His hip jiggled to some beat only he could hear, setting some chains swinging from his belt -- also good, sturdy leather with a wicked-looking buckle. He stroked his hand down tight thighs, letting Clay get a good look at the two leather bracelets he wore.

Without any clue as to what he should say, except *why the hell are* you *doing speed dating?* Clay stared at Michael and waited for him to make the first move.

Silence dragged on between them.

"Come here often?" Clay cracked after a minute or so of the staring contest.

Michael nodded.

Okay, it was a start. Clay spread his hands wide. "So. See anything you like?"

Michael eyed Clay up and down, then narrowed his eyes and nodded. Miracle of miracles, he opened his mouth and spoke. "Do you want to get out of here?"

"Excuse me?" Clay blinked.

"Out of here, you and me." Michael looked impatient. "I've got the afternoon off and the apartment to myself."

Oh, that's *tempting.* Sad thing was, it actually kind of was enticing. Underneath the spikes and the eye makeup, Michael had a sharply attractive face that would have been stunning and drawn every eye, no jewelry necessary.

"I don't exactly do…" Clay started to demur.

"Why? You scared?"

Clay's head snapped up. "Okay. Thank you for coming by," he rapped out sharply. One finger reached for and unerringly hit the button for Jeri. "Hey, sweetie?" he called. "Next one up, okay?"

"This is only used as a panic button," Jeri chirped.

"Call this an emergency." Michael leered at Clay and adjusted himself in his frighteningly tight leather pants. "There's a definite urgency to the situation."

"Your loss," Michael said, standing up. He offered his hand to Clay, who, startled, took it. A piece of paper was suddenly nestling in his palm. "My number," Michael said, tossing Clay a wink. "In case you change your mind. Any time you want some action, give me a call."

Clay nodded weakly, awash in Michael's sea of testosterone, then hammered on the button. "Jeri? Next. Next!"

* * *

"Hey, friend. The name's Adam." The short, muscled man swung the dating service's chair around and sat in it backwards. Arms crossed on the back, he leaned his chin into their support and grinned at Clay. "How's it going?"

Clay, still reeling a little from his experience with Michael, shook his head twice before the words sank in. Relaxing, he reached out to grasp Adam's hand. Ooh. Hard and calloused. This was a guy who worked for his living. Worked hard, probably. Those muscles didn't come from any health club.

And he did love a good strong man. Even if the man in question happened to stand a few inches shorter than him. Close to six, but who was he to judge? "I'm Clay," he said with a grin. "So, what's a nice guy like you doing in a place like this?"

Adam laughed, albeit a little ruefully. "Funny thing," he said. "The more open society gets about guys like us, the harder it is to find a date. Especially if you're not twenty and built like a brick shithouse, you know?"

Clay rolled his eyes and nodded. "God, tell me about it. I had this little blond guy, barely legal, tell me he wasn't interested because I didn't have a six-pack and my hair was messy."

"Did you go out and buy a case of beer?" Adam joked.

"Wiseass." Clay grinned. "Nah, but I did get someone to tell me what a six-pack was. Then I went to work and grew my own."

"Yeah? Not bad. Can I see?"

Clay blinked, but then again, what the hell? Untucking his T-shirt, he raised it so that Adam could cop an eyeful of his midsection. The man nodded, definitely approving, then raised his own loose T-shirt to show off a chest that put Clay's to shame. Yeah. Definitely a guy who did some seriously hard work for his living.

Hey, he wasn't a snob. Nothing wrong with a good blue-collar guy if he'd be faithful and come home at night instead of going out with the boys. Clay nodded appreciatively at the sight of Adam with his shirt half off. His cock gave a slight twitch, as if to say that it approved, too.

"Now that we've shaken hands and beat our breasts, what happens next?" Adam asked.

"You don't know?"

"Nope. This is my first time in the joint. I'm a virgin." Adam winked. "Treat me gentle, big boy. What do you feel like we should do?"

Clay shifted, feeling the crinkle of Michael's phone number in his pocket. "You seem like a nice guy," he said honestly. "What do you like to do? What do you do? For a living, I mean."

"Mechanic." Adam held up his hands, grimacing at the dark dirt that had worked its way into the cracks on the skin. "I work down at the auto plant. But when I'm not on the job, I love going down to this pool hall close to the beach."

"You're good?"

"Damned good." Adam gave a grin that almost stopped Clay's heart. God, the man was gorgeous when he smiled. "You and me, let's play a game sometime, huh? Doesn't matter if it's a date or just two guys hanging out."

"It doesn't? Matter, I mean?"

Adam shrugged, getting up. "People told me this speed dating thing was nuts," he said frankly. "I figured it'd be a way to meet people, you know? Folks who aren't all about cars or how many bottles of beer they can drink before they forget their crappy day. You and me, I think we could get along. Even if you don't like what you see enough to sleep with it, maybe we can have a few laughs." He pulled a slip of paper out of his chest pocket. "Here. My number. You ever feel like shooting a game, give me a call."

With that, he turned his back and headed for the door. Clay half-stood, wanting to ask Adam to stay. Gorgeous, and friendly to boot. Still… something stopped him. He wasn't sure what, but when Adam turned around to give him a good-bye grin, Clay didn't ask him to stay. Instead, he waved as the man left.

Then, somehow uncomfortable, he slumped down at the table. He could hear Jeri outside, bidding Adam goodbye. Another good guy, a could-have-been. Why hadn't he jumped at the man?

Slowly, Clay slid the phone number into his pocket. It nestled against Michael's, feeling like two strikes against him.

What would happen with the third?

* * *

If Adam had been short, the next guy who came in the door was large enough to make

Clay's eyes bug out briefly. So tall he had to duck through, and just about as broad. Muscles like they didn't make outside of horses, arms like knotted wood, and legs like beer barrels. Workout queen? Clay couldn't tell.

The big guy turned the chair Adam had sat in back around and plunked himself on it. The wood gave an ominous creak, but no untoward accidents happened. He offered Clay a hand as big as a plate and grinned. "Name's Jefferson," he said. "So you're Clay, right?"

Clay nodded, wincing a little as Jefferson squeezed his hand. Jesus! He wasn't any ninety-pound weakling, but a grip like that could bend steel. "That'd be me."

Jefferson spread his hands. "So, here I am. You want to check out the goods?"

"Uh, isn't that kind of my job? You're the one here to try and score with me."

The big guy cracked up. "All right, point for you. You're the first guy who hasn't started stumbling and stammering when I laid that line on them." He leaned forward, amiable as a tame grizzly bear. "Look, here's the thing. I'm fuckin' huge, right? So I intimidate people. That's why I do things like this speed dating service. I've been hunting for someone who isn't too put off by the size to think about tak-ing on the whole package."

Clay grinned. "Got to admit, as plans go that one isn't bad. How many times have you gotten lucky?"

Jefferson's eyes grew warm. "As of now? Once."

"Oh." Clay drew back a little, but then, remembering himself, settled into an easy pose on his chair. "Yeah, you are a bruiser. How'd you get that way? Luck of the genetic draw, or maybe working out?"

"Six of one, half dozen of the other." Jefferson shrugged. "If a guy my height lets himself run to fat, I'd end up not being able to fit through doorways. More than I already don't, that is." He winced. "Man, the number of times I've whacked my head on lintels, let me tell you."

"Lintels?"

"Yeah. You know, the top of a doorway." Jefferson made a gesture to indicate what he meant, then gave Clay a suspicious eye. "Say, what do you do for a living?"

"Radio DJ," Clay answered, no apologies.

"You ever do trivia contests?"

"On occasion."

"And you didn't know that?"

"As a matter of fact, no." Clay found he was enjoying himself, batting questions and answers back and forth between himself and this mountain of a man. "What do you do, Jefferson?"

White teeth flashed in Jefferson's tanned face. "I teach architecture at the local college."

"Oh, now see, you cheated." Clay reached out to shove Jefferson. Felt like pushing at a brick wall, but Jefferson laughed and swatted back -- thankfully, pulling his punch. Clay grinned, sizing the guy up. He couldn't imagine himself in bed with this man without being crushed, but he had a way about him that made Clay want to get to know him better.

A *ting* sounded from the timer. Clay gave it a dismayed glance. Their time was almost up already? "Got a phone number?" he asked, trying not to sound desperate. Didn't want to give Jefferson the wrong idea. "Maybe we could get together some time and go running."

"On the beach?" Jefferson challenged, pulling a slip out of his hip pocket.

Clay took it, feeling the warmth of the paper. "Best kind of workout, running in the water," he came back. "I'm game if you are."

Jefferson looked him up and down, then gave a nod and another one of those rich smiles. "You're all right, Clay. Maybe we can get to know each other better."

"I'd like that," Clay said honestly. He reached out to shake again, wincing when the buzzer interrupted their contact. "Just friends, though. For now," he amended.

Jefferson looked a little disappointed, but nodded. "You got it, man," he said jovially. "Who knows what can happen with a little bit of time?"

"Who knows?" Clay sat back in his chair as Jefferson made his way to the door. He had to duck under the lintel again, but he managed to wave back at Clay as he exited.

The intercom buzzed, startling Clay. "Jeri?"

"You're done for the day, sugar," Jeri said in her whiskey-smooth tones. "Three's the limit. Just like in a bar."

"I think it's two in a bar."

"You'd know better than I would," she said archly. "I have my man to go home to." Her voice turned secretive and interested. "So? Did you find a Prince Charming today?"

Clay thought back over the men he'd visited with. Michael, gorgeous but weird. Adam, short, but as open and friendly as a good summer day. Jefferson, a challenge in every sense of the word. "I met three very different guys," he said. "I have to say there was a certain something about each one of them. Hell, even the first contestant had some potential."

"No winners, though, huh?"

"I got three phone numbers. Does that count?"

"It's a start, sweetie. Now you get off your duff and go home. Make some calls tonight and see what happens!"

"Yeah," Clay said absently. "I might just do that. But would you put me down for another session, say, tomorrow afternoon? Just one more."

"Just like a man," Jeri tsked. "You have to squeeze all the fruit before you decide what's ripe."

Clay's mind's eye flashed on a vision of Adam's taut, tight buttocks in his hard-worn jeans. He cleared his throat. "Something like that. One more, tomorrow?"

"You've got it. Be here at ten a.m. Now, clear out of that room. We're busy today, and there's someone else just waiting for their chance to meet Mr. Right. Chop, chop!" Jeri clapped her hands together.

Nothing left to do, Clay got up and pushed his chair back in. He headed back out the door he'd come in, exiting into the outside world. Alone.

* * *

How long Clay stood there in the parking lot of the dating service, he couldn't have said afterwards. The salt breezes blew through his hair, mussing it even further and tangling it into elf-knots that would be a bitch to comb out later. He felt like there was something missing, but he couldn't have said what it was.

No amount of self-examination was giving him any answers -- that was until, impatient with himself, he reached for his car keys.

He stared at them, lying warm in his palm, his mind's eye flashing back to the Post-it note they'd been wrapped up in that morning. Clutching them lightly, then tightly, Clay sighed. Yeah. Michael, Adam, and Jefferson had all been great guys -- okay, maybe not Michael. He could have hooked up with either A or J, though, no problem. So why hadn't he?

The answer lay in his palm. Seth. He hadn't wanted any of them because none of them were Seth. Seth, the straight man. Seth, the guy who was even bad at pretending to be gay.

Seth, who didn't love Clay the way Clay loved him.

Closing his hand into a tight fist, Clay raised himself away from the sun-warmed bricks of the building and headed for his car. He'd take Jeri's advice. Go home, make a few phone calls that night, at least two, and see what he could set in motion. A game of pool with Adam, a run with Jefferson. He was two friends richer, three if you counted good-time Mikey, and hey, who didn't want to have a good time every now and then?

If the thought left a taste like ashes in his mouth, that was his own affair.

He started to unlock his car, the key halfway into the slot, when he heard -- "You!" The shout was all the warning he had before two small fists had grabbed him and slung him around with his back against the hood, his face toward the Wrath of Sophie.

"What the hell?" Clay struggled to stand back up. "Why are you here?"

"I saw your car." Sophie kicked at a tire with one daintily sandaled foot. "No one else drives a P.O.S. like this. It just screams 'Clay'. You know, I bet this was once a nice automobile, until you drove it into the ground."

"Living near the ocean is hell on a vehicle, Sophie." Clay tried to edge away from the small woman, not liking the look in her fierce blue eyes. "So, you found me. What do you want?"

"What do I -- oh, that's rich." Sophie almost laughed. "I want my boyfriend back, you thief."

"You what, now?" Clay sputtered. "Oh! Seth. You want Seth back? That's why you're assaulting me in a public place?"

Sophie kicked him hard on the shin. "There! Now it's assault." She stood back, folding her arms. "Are you going to have me arrested?"

When Clay shook his head, she tossed her hair, silky golden waves falling down around her shoulders. "I want Seth back," she said warningly. "If you don't hand him over, I'm going to make both of your lives hell."

Clay closed his eyes against an incipient headache. It wasn't that he didn't think Sophie could do it, but it was more than he couldn't face up to her at the moment. "I can't give Seth back," he said quietly. "He's not mine to give or take."

"But you did take him!" Sophie socked him in the chest. "There! Aggravated assault. Do you want to call the cops on me?"

"Jesus, no. Would you calm down?"

"I'm calm as ice." Belying her words, Sophie's eyes blazed. "I just want to make sure we understand each other. You let Seth go, and send him back to me. Otherwise, you pay. Am I being clear?"

"Crystal. But Sophie, he's a grown man. You can't tell him what to do."

"Oh, really?" Sophie turned to stalk away. "I have, I can, and I will. He just needs to see that he belongs with me. Give me time, Clay. And give him back." She turned to glare over one honeyed shoulder. "Did you ever honestly think you could make him happy?"

Clay found he didn't have a single thing to say. Not one word hopped onto his tongue. Frankly, there wasn't anything he could have added. Seth wouldn't have been happy with him, so Sophie was right. But send him back to this crazy bitch? No way.

"He's better off," Clay surprised himself by shouting. Sophie froze in place, shooting daggers at Clay. "He is. He's happier now. You should see him. With me. He can be himself. And he's a good man, Sophie. Do you want him back if all he's going to be is miserable?"

Sophie glared a moment longer, then turned on her heel and clacked away. Clay leaned against his car, staring after her. He shivered. God, no wonder he was gay. Women were insane! How had she found him, anyway? Driving around, his ass. She'd been hunting him.

Hunting…

"Oh, God," Clay muttered. "Seth." He jammed the keys into the door lock, flung it open, and hurled himself into the car, barely pausing for his seatbelt before peeling out of the parking lot.

Whatever the hell she had done to Seth, she was going to regret it.

Chapter Eight

Seth lay down on the soft blanket spread across springy grass, let out a deep breath, and gazed up at the sky. The sound of waves and seagulls filled his ears, lulling him into a sense of serenity. He was grateful for it -- after a day like his, he needed all the peace he could get. There was just something about watching the sun set over the ocean which made a man forget all his cares and woes.

Clay's feet came into vision, treading close to Seth's ear. He turned, examining them idly. For a guy, he had nice feet. Big, sure, but smooth and tanned. Good ankles, too, tapering up into strong legs.

"Hey," Seth said quietly.

"Hey, yourself." Clay replied. "Is there brooding space on this blanket for two, or should I go somewhere else?"

"There's room," Seth's mouth said before his brain caught up. Ye gods. The last thing he should have wanted was Clay getting close and cozy -- wasn't it? Clay plus close equaled greater confusion, and he'd come outside to get his head straightened out. Thing was, he couldn't say no. He couldn't deny Clay anything, he realized.

Clay was looking at him doubtfully, as if he didn't quite believe Seth. "Come on," Seth urged, now that the deed had been done. He scooted over a few inches, feeling the soft sedge beneath his back. "Have a seat."

There was a pause, and then Clay nodded. "Thanks." He crossed over Seth and folded down Indian-style on the blanket. A bottle of juice in his hand glistened with condensation. "You want some?"

Seth considered the notion. "Yeah. Thanks."

The bottle was passed over, and Seth sipped. Pomegranate. Not his favorite, but it had a tart bite that his tongue appreciated. Just sweet enough to combat the sourness. "It's good," he said, wiping off the mouth of the bottle before passing it back over.

Clay took a swig. "Not bad," he agreed. Dangling the neck between two fingers, he let it hang between his knees. "Kinda sour."

"That's how it's supposed to taste."

"Catch me listening to Anthony's recommendations again, then."

Seth winced. Then, pushing Anthony from his mind, he concentrated on the sound of the waves. Rushing in, ebbing out. He envisioned himself walking across the salty, hard-packed sand, his feet leaving tracks that the water filled as he passed by.

He envisioned a scene out of "From Here To Eternity", starring himself and Clay, and winced again. Okay, point one, he didn't have a clue as to what two guys did together. Two, who said Clay would be interested? Three, did he want to play those games himself?

"Pass the juice back over," Seth grumbled. The cool bottle pressed into his hands. He took a long swig, savoring the tart burst of flavor over his tongue. It woke up the brain, kept it from falling into daydreams that would only end in tears. So to speak. He was a guy and he didn't cry all that often. A hammer to the thumb might produce a drop or two, but not something like this.

Right?

"Did you make the grocery list?" Clay asked idly, taking his juice back. "We're out of most of the basics. Eggs, bread, milk, cereal..."

"What? Oh. Nah, I forgot." Seth tipped Clay a rueful smile. "Been a lot of things going on the past few days."

"Understood, and forgiven." Clay stretched out his long legs. "Okay, compose it in your head for later. Bananas, sugar, chicken, tea bags, and fresh vegetables. Carrots, peppers, onions. A cut of stew beef. I'll make us something in the Crock-Pot. Good and juicy, something for both of us to come home to."

"Pasta," Seth chipped in. "Rigatoni and ziti. Maybe some of those little shells."

"Red sauce? Marinara?"

"Nah. I like the alfredo."

"You would."

The conversation ebbed back into silence again, each thinking about things they weren't sharing with one another. At least Seth wasn't.

"So, how did it go at the speed dating agency?" he asked to fill the silence. Seth knew he never had been good at the awkward pause thing. All the same, he wanted to bite his lip the moment the words escaped his mouth.

Clay shrugged. "Not too bad. Met a scary Goth kid and a couple of nice guys."

Seth felt a twinge of jealousy that he tried, briefly, to analyze, before giving a snort. "Nice as in you wanted to go out with them?"

"I got one invitation to go play pool, and one to run on the beach. Man, you should have seen this fellow. I don't think I've ever seen anyone that tall or built. He dwarfed me."

Seth cast an incredulous eye at Clay. At six feet tall and well-muscled, it was hard to imagine anyone who could make him feel little. "You're joking."

"My hand to God. This guy could have stepped on me." Clay shifted, then lay back on the blanket to stare at the sky himself. "Pretty," he commented idly. "I think sunset is my favorite time of day."

"You don't like sunrises?"

"Hard to, when I usually prefer to sleep through them." Clay elbowed Seth, who had to laugh.

"Okay, fair enough." Seth shifted. "So, are you going to take either one of these Romeos up on their offer?"

Clay shuffled, then gave an abbreviated shrug. "Maybe. I have one more session at the agency tomorrow. If I don't find Mr. Perfect then, could be I'll go off with Adam or Jefferson." He paused, considering. "Probably Adam. I liked his attitude. Totally upfront about everything, and he understood what it was like not to be a perfect ten."

"Not to be a -- what are you talking about?" Seth twisted his head to stare at Clay. "You're saying you're not?"

Clay laughed. "Me? Not hardly. For one thing, I'm too old."

"Barely thirty."

"That's nine years too old. I have dark hair, I don't surf, and when I try to dance I look like I'm having a seizure. Doesn't make for popularity among the young and hung." Clay sighed. "The older you get, the harder it is."

Seth frowned, mulling that over. "So you had a lot of dates when you were younger?"

"I had my share." Clay stretched his legs, arching his toes. "About average, I guess. Sometimes I had to sneak around. You know. First I wasn't out, and then there were guys who weren't out themselves. Took a while before I found someone who didn't mind admitting who he was."

Ah. Seth squirmed guiltily. Unconsciously, he edged an inch or so closer to Clay. Nervousness threatened to overwhelm him, but honestly, who else could he ask? "So... when did you know you were gay?" he blurted in a rush.

He saw Clay turn his head to stare at him. "Why do you want to know?"

The voice held no hostility, just honest curiosity. Seth took courage from Clay's openness and went on. "You don't have to tell me if you don't want. I'm just trying to understand this whole thing. Maybe it'd help if you told me when you'd figured it out."

Clay looked thoughtful. "If you want to go back to the basics, around when I hit puberty," he said absently. "Other guys were noticing girls, and I was noticing guys. Breasts did nothing for me, no matter how much the boys talked about them. Then, when they started going on about kissing and scoring, it just left me cold."

"What then?" Seth pressed. "Did you meet someone, or...?"

"Or," Clay chuckled. "I found a magazine some kids had been passing around. Blue as a sailor's shirt. They'd been treating it like a joke, but after the teacher confiscated the thing, I broke into her desk drawer and smuggled it home with me.

"I can still remember it now," he said, long fingers drifting over his chest. "Glossy photos of guys kissing guys, sucking cock, even a shot of one man doing another. They were every- where -- in the sun, underneath a waterfall, even, surprisingly enough, in a bed." He paused. "I looked at those men for hours be- fore I realized that was what I wanted to do. To be. After that, it was a matter of figuring out what to call myself."

"Gay," Seth supplied. His stomach felt tight.

"You know it. Want more juice?"

Seth shifted. "No, thanks. Have you ever… you know, with a girl…" Seth paused.

"God, no!" Clay burst into laughter. "I might wonder from time to time, but I've never had sex with a woman. I don't think I'd know where to start. Not like you." He nudged Seth. The touch felt playful. "How many women have you slept with?"

Seth squirmed. "I don't know, so much…"

"Lost track?"

"Somewhere along the line," Seth lied. It had actually been fifteen, but the last thing he wanted was for Clay to think he just put it out there for anyone to take. But then again, why didn't he want that? "Sophie being the last, and of the longest duration."

"Stamina, huh?"

"What? Oh, no. I meant, she hung around for months. Most women, they figured out I was just a beach bum with delusions of gran- deur and took off for greener pastures. Didn't take them very long. Sophie, though, she had plans." Seth grimaced. "I can't believe she tracked me down today."

"Tracked you -- you're kidding me. You, too?"

"She came after you?" Seth rolled over onto his stomach, staring at Clay. "Jesus, man. Did she do anything to you?"

"Just shot off her mouth." Clay shrugged. "I got worried about you, but when I got home and you were playing games on the computer, I didn't figure I needed to say anything. But she accosted you? When? How?"

"I went out to breakfast with Anthony. Sophie found me in the Seaside Diner." Seth waved it aside as unimportant, then paused. He elbowed Clay. "You know, she had a preacher with her?"

Clay had just taken a sip of juice. He choked. "A preacher? What the hell for?"

"Apparently, he was with one of those gay de-programming units," Seth admitted. "She was going to reconvert me. All I had to do was go along like a good little boy."

"Oh, that's low. What did you do?"

Seth shifted again. He couldn't exactly see himself confessing to Clay: *I told her that I loved you, and I didn't have any plans to re-train myself like a good little puppy, so the preacher could go get impaled on a pitchfork and she should go back home to her spider web.*

"Nothing much," he fibbed. "I just told them I wasn't interested."

"Pretty emphatically, I bet."

"You could say that. Juice?"

Clay passed the bottle over, but instead of giving it hand to hand, he slowly rolled the bottle down Seth's forearm, nestling it into his palm. Seth shivered, and not just from the cold. "I'm proud of you," Clay said softly. "I know what kind of guts it took to tell her off."

Seth clutched the bottle. "It wasn't a big deal," he protested, voice low. "I -- she's -- I'm not interested in her anymore."

"So what are you interested in?" Clay sounded unbearably patient. "All these questions about being gay, Seth. Are you maybe thinking about going after someone?"

"No!" Seth blurted. Then, he sighed. "Maybe? I don't know."

"Who?"

As if I'd tell Clay! Hey, I have a crush on you. Here's hoping it doesn't ruin our friendship, but would you mind showing me a few things about how guys get down and dirty together? Yeah. That *would go over really well.*

"Just someone I met the other day." The lies were stacking higher and higher. And did he imagine it, or did Clay look disappointed at the words? Seth's heart beat faster. What if… what if he did come clean? Tell Clay everything?

Slowly, shyly, not quite believing he was doing it, Seth reached out. His fingers inched across the blanket until they touched Clay's. He took the big hand in his own and squeezed hard. "I'm confused, Clay," he admitted. "This all started off as a big game, and now I don't know which way to turn."

Clay hadn't drawn back. Carefully, he stroked Seth's hand with his thumb. A long moment of silence passed between them, Seth's heart pounding in his throat. Finally, Clay spoke.

"You asked me to show you how all of this worked," he said quietly. "If you really want to know what it's all about, I'll take it a step further."

Seth swallowed hard. "You'd...?"

"Why not? It'd be the same as when Anthony and I get together." Clay's thumb made smooth sweeps over Seth's hand. "Just friends, indulging a little curiosity. If it's what you want, I can help you out. It's not like you're hard to look at."

Seth felt himself turning pink, something he hadn't done in ages. "You -- you think I'm good-looking?"

Clay chuckled. "I do have eyes, man. You're a pretty fine specimen of manhood. Not that I've ever been perving on you or anything. Just noticing in passing, so to speak."

Seth felt an extra twinge of guilt. "And you'd show me? I mean, I guess I need to know. Whether or not I like things, I mean."

"Would it help?"

"Might give me a hand on making up my mind." Seth ran his tongue across his lips, which felt dry, as if he'd been eating the pomegranates instead of drinking their juice. "How do we start?"

"For one thing, you relax." Clay squeezed Seth's hand back. "Just lie back and relax, okay? If I do anything you don't like, just say so. No means no, right?"

"Right." Seth wiggled with nervousness. He couldn't believe he was about to -- but he'd asked for it, hadn't he? "Go ahead."

"I already am." Clay applied a gentle pressure to Seth's fingers. "We're holding hands. Touching digits is as good a place to start as any."

"Oh?" Seth struggled for calmness and some degree of cool. "That's okay, then. I mean, this is cool."

"Good. Now just lie still, okay? Let me do all the work."

Seth shifted uncomfortably. Words like those were supposed to be *his* line, coaxing a date into letting him go a little further. All the same, he trusted Clay. The man wouldn't go too far. Slowly, he nodded.

"Okay," Clay breathed. "Don't say anything unless you want me to stop. Just enjoy this. Just feel."

Ever so slowly, Clay freed his hand from Seth's. He ghosted it up the length of Seth's arm, barely touching the skin. Seth felt the small hairs on his arm tingling, as if he were being caressed by a ghost. The sensation sent shivers down his spine, but he liked them.

Clay's hand moved again, this time over Seth's chest. Using one forefinger, he drew a line down Seth's chest to his stomach. He ran that finger along the edge of Seth's T-shirt. "Can I?" he whispered.

Don't say a word, Seth reminded himself. He took a deep breath and nodded.

"Thank you," Clay murmured. Ever so gently, he raised Seth's T-shirt up, the material drifting away from him. Seth shuddered as the cooling night air touched his skin, all the way up to his nipples. "Will you take this off?"

Seth nodded. Sitting up a little, he let Clay peel the shirt off him. Then, as if he weighed no more than a feather, Clay laid him back down on the blanket. "Just lie there," Clay's voice soothed. "Close your eyes."

Obediently, Seth shut them. He wanted to see, but at the same time, he didn't want anything to interfere with the pure sensations washing over him. Salt air and Clay's hands. Hands stroking up and down his chest, and then fingers on his nipples. Not pinching or pulling, just rubbing slow circles around them. Seth was startled by how good the sensation felt, and tried to express his appreciation by arching up into Clay's touch.

Clay chuckled. "Now, remember you can say no at any time," he reminded Seth. Then, suddenly, Seth's left nipple was surrounded by wet warmth. He felt a tongue lashing at his skin, and gentle suction being applied.

He couldn't help letting a moan escape. The feel of Clay's hands on him and that warm suckling felt better than almost anything. His cock began to get hard, rising and filling in his shorts. He didn't freak out, though, although for a second it was a near thing.

Just feel, he reminded himself. *It's okay. This is just Clay. My friend.*

When the mouth left his nipple, he almost whimpered. Clay stroked his skin, murmuring nonsense that soothed him down. "Lie still," he said clearly. "Let me do this."

Seth held absolutely firm in place. Or at least he did until he felt the lips on his cheek. Light as Clay's earlier touch, sweeter than any-thing he'd ever felt. They ghosted from one side to the other, then kissed the tip of his nose, then his chin, then his forehead. Seth's dick surged upward harder as his heartbeat sped up, anticipating…

Yes. Gentle as a breeze, Clay's lips fastened over his own. Seth lay frozen. His second real kiss with a man. Time seemed to stand still.

Slowly, Clay traced Seth's lips with the tip of his tongue. Automatically, Seth's mouth opened before he realized what he was doing. Clay made a small, nonverbal growl, and slid his tongue inside. Noises regardless, he was still gentle, stroking Seth's tongue with his own, as if he were gently making love to Seth's mouth. It seemed like Clay was putting all his effort into making this feel good.

And it did, or at least it wasn't freaking Seth out. Cautiously, he stretched out with his own tongue and twined it around Clay's. He tasted like pomegranates, sweet and sour. Wasn't there some old legend about tasting those fruits and then falling? *Persephone*, he thought hazily, before he was lost in the kiss.

Seth had no idea how long it went on, a simple touch of mouth to mouth, and tongue to tongue, but when Clay's hand began to move again he jumped. Clay drew back instantly. "Too much?" he asked. "All you have to do is say stop."

Opening his eyes to the darkening sky, Seth discovered that everything looked hazy. He shook his head. The whole of his body was trembling, his cock was hard enough that it hurt, and the last thing he wanted was for Clay to stop, even if this was all for pretend.

"Okay," Clay murmured, kissing Seth's lips again ever so briefly. "This is one of the things that men do together."

He trailed a row of kisses down Seth's chest, stopping at the waistband of his shorts. "Too much?" he asked, fingers already slipping underneath the elastic.

Seth didn't answer in words. Instead, hands shaking, he laid them over Clay's hands and squeezed. *Go ahead. I want you to.*

"All right," Clay whispered. Ever so slowly, inch by inch, he peeled down Seth's shorts. When Seth's cock popped out into the cool night air, Seth couldn't help a small groan of relief.

"Easy, easy," Clay soothed.

Is he going to? Is he going to? Seth babbled in his own mind as Clay nuzzled the small trail of hair on his chest. *Come on, please, let him do it. I'm not freaking out, which should freak me all the more, but I'm not. I actually want him to do this. I'm aching for the feel of his lips on my cock, where no one but women have been before.*

Is it too soon for this? Is it too much to ask Clay? What if he doesn't want to? What if I'm pushing him?

Seth opened his eyes again and glanced down the length of his body. What he saw took his breath away. Clay's head, dark and shaggy, poised over his dick. His own cock, standing thick and tall, ridged with veins, dark with blood, and pulsing slightly. The sight sent a jolt of pleasure through him, and a bead of pre-come bubbled out of his slit.

"It's okay," Clay soothed, rubbing small circles on Seth's stomach. "I'll stop if you say so."

Seth took a deep breath and shook his head no. He didn't know why, but he wanted this more than anything ever before in his life. The thought of Clay's mouth surrounding him filled his veins with fire. Another shock of delight rippled through him, releasing another bead of clear fluid.

Clay lowered his mouth to Seth's cock. His tongue came out and curled around the tip, dabbing up the drips of pre-come. Seth couldn't help giving a loud moan, arching his back. The heat, the slickness, the knowledge that this was *Clay* about to give him head…

"More?" Clay whispered.

Seth nodded eagerly.

"You asked for it, then," Clay said. He kissed the tip of Seth's cock again, and then carefully slid the organ into his mouth. Seth almost forgot how to breathe as Clay worked his way down the shaft. This was unbelievable. He'd had blow jobs before, sure, but they were from women acting like they were doing him an incredible favor. They loved it when he went down on them, sure, but when it came to playing turnabout? No deal.

Not Clay. He loved to suck cock, and it showed. The lashing of his tongue sent a third surge through Seth, who began to take deep breaths in an effort to steady himself. Clay's hands kneaded his thighs, telling him silently that it was okay, that this was a lot to deal with all at once.

Clay didn't stop with just tongue-play. As Seth watched, Clay's cheeks hollowed out and he felt the most incredible suction on his dick. The sight blew his mind, and he was afraid that his balls would follow. They were already drawing up tight to his body, and the sensation, the burning need to come, was only increased when Clay freed one hand to cup and roll them. He knew just how to do it, too, hard enough that he could feel something, but lightly enough that it didn't hurt.

Seth heard a low moaning sound, and realized that it was him. Clay petted him again, as if promising things were okay. He could let go if he wanted -- he could --

Then Clay swallowed, and Seth lost control. Giving a sharp shout, he raised his hips in his orgasm and felt pulse after pulse of seed burst from the tip of his dick. Clay's tongue was there right away, licking up the dribbles that escaped, swallowing them down. As Seth panted, trying to put his brain back together, Clay sucked gently, cleaning him up.

Then he was pulling off, and it was over. Seth's head felt loose on his neck. He stared up at Clay, who was carefully pulling Seth's shorts back up.

"That's what it's all about," he said softly. "Or at least as much as I think you're ready for right now."

Seth's body burned. He wanted -- something more. Thing was, he didn't know what. A kiss, maybe? The idea of tasting himself on Clay's lips sent a surge of heat to his lower belly, and he began to raise up, wanting to touch the man's mouth with his own --

Clay's hand on his chest stopped him. "Not yet," he said, his eyes tinged with a sort of sadness. "That was for you, not me. I'm not taking anything you're not ready to give yet. Really ready. Just cope with what we've done, and then maybe we'll talk tomorrow."

As Seth watched in disbelief, Clay stood, grabbing his juice bottle. He lay unable to move while the man who'd just given him the sweetest blow job of his life walked away, heading for the house they shared.

At the doorway, Clay paused and turned around. "It's not about being gay," he offered quietly. "It's about caring for the person you're with. Maybe you need to consider that, Seth. Then, ask me some more questions about what it's like to live as a gay man."

And with that, he was gone, disappearing inside. Seth stared for a moment, then collapsed back onto the blanket. The waves sounded louder in his ears, until he realized it was his own blood pressure roaring. His throat was parched dry, his body hummed with satisfaction, and yet he wanted more. What, he wasn't sure, but just -- more.

Slowly, he stretched out his arms and legs like a starfish, as if he were making snow angels, and let them slide back and forth. Did he have any of his questions answered? He wasn't sure. His first gay sexual experience, and it had been wonderful, but it left him aching in ways he'd never experienced before.

It's about who you're with, Clay's voice echoed in Seth's head. Seth closed his eyes and imagined Clay over him again, those dark eyes warm with lust and tenderness.

"Clay," he whispered, testing and tasting the name on his tongue. "Clay, I think I'm falling for you."

But his words were lost in the roaring of the surf. And he didn't know that inside, Clay was leaning against a wall, face buried in his arms, sobbing as if his heart were about to break. Thumping the plaster with a fist, muttering words under his breath, and fighting against the urge to run back outside and take Seth where he lay.

Seth had no idea. And so he lay underneath the stars, awash with sexual satisfaction, his mind roaming over curiosity after curiosity. Peace tugged at him, and he sighed, shutting his eyes. Sleep wasn't far away, and it'd be nice to spend the night underneath the stars…

And before he knew it, he was asleep.

Not knowing that inside the house, Clay was dialing the phone…

Chapter Nine

"It'll be okay, baby." Anthony's slim arms wrapped around Clay's back, pulling him in close. He tucked his head into the curve of his friend's shoulder, smelling the fragrant shampoo he used and the indescribable scent that belonged only to him. He felt one small hand petting the back of his head as Anthony crooned, and closed his eyes.

With Anthony, just for a moment, he could pretend he hadn't just made the single biggest mistake of his adult life.

"Whatever's wrong, we'll work it out," Anthony was promising as he rocked Clay. Despite the difference in their sizes, he managed it pretty handily.

Must be the mothering instinct he drags out from time to time, especially when I've put my foot in it, Clay thought, clinging tightly. "You have no idea how deep I'm in this time," he muttered against Anthony's soft skin.

"How bad is it?"

"Eyeball level and sinking fast."

"Oh, Clay." Anthony released him and stood back, taking his hands. "What did you do? Is it Seth?"

Clay drew in a deep breath which was, apparently, all Anthony needed to hear. "Okay, come inside. This requires serious bonding time. I'll put on some coffee. You go through to the art patch and check out my latest while I brew." With one hand, he stroked back a tangle of Clay's hair. "Sometimes I don't know why I love you so much," he said frankly. "Right about then, you usually remind me. So go in there and start getting your story ready. I want to hear every word of it."

"All right." Clay knew he sounded gravelly. He cleared his throat and nodded. Anthony cupped his cheek for a moment, then smiled at him. "I really did screw up," he confessed.

"I know you did. So we'll fix it. Now, scoot."

Clay scooted. Anthony's apartment, really more of a studio, had sections blocked off by elaborate rice-paper screens of his own design. To get to the sunniest space by the windows, where Anthony painted, Clay had to weave his way through a tangle of den, library, storage room, and finally a new partition, set up with a cat tree and a litter box.

"Don't tell me you're going to get a kitten," he called back to the kitchen area, where he could hear Anthony puttering around with jars of instant and a canister of cream.

Spoons tinkled as Anthony called back to Clay, "Already got one! Be careful you don't step on him. He's kind of skittish. You probably scared him underneath something when you knocked on the door."

"What kind of cat?" Clay picked his way with extra caution, watching for any waving tails underneath furniture. "Regular old American stew, or a purebred?"

"Vintage supermarket box breed. I think he's half Siamese. All the points, but white paws." Anthony clanked and clunked a little more. "I actually had the coffee out earlier. Have you ever seen a kitten drink the stuff? Add a drop of it to his milk, and he goes to town."

"I don't actually think you're supposed to give kittens cow's milk," Clay said, finally making his way to the art "room". Two paint-spattered stools sat empty, one drawn up in front of a half-finished canvas. He examined the painting with curiosity. Looked like Anthony was trying to copy the weird old sunflowers masterpiece, with the addition of a foxy little feline weaving his way in and out of the stalks. "True love, huh?"

"Sometimes it happens." Anthony appeared with a tray full of cups, sugar cubes, and a carton of half-and-half. "Besides, it was soy."

The non sequitur took Clay by surprise. "Say what now?"

"What I fed the kitty. His name's Raku. Soy milk, not cow's."

Clay eyed the carton on their coffee tray. "And this is…"

"Good old Bessie's best. Don't be so skittish." Anthony plopped down on the stool next to the canvas, and gestured for Clay to take a seat. "Okay, the doctor is in. Tell me all about it. What did you do?"

Clay dragged in a deep breath. "It's bad, Toni."

He nodded thoughtfully. "Okay. It's bad, it has to do with Seth, and you smell like sex. For some reason, these facts aren't adding up in my mind. Want to start at the beginning and see how far we get?"

"I blew him," Clay admitted, head downcast. "We were out in the backyard. He'd been asking all these questions about what gay men like to do, and he grabbed my hand. Swear, Anthony, it felt just like electricity. I couldn't have stopped myself if I'd tried."

"Did you try?"

"No," he admitted, staring at the cup Anthony passed him. "He was asking for me to touch him. Really asking, not just playing around. I kept stopping to check if this was all too much, but he pushed me further and further until I just… I did what I did. I gave him a blow job."

"Mmm." Clay heard Anthony take a delicate sip of his coffee. "How did he react?"

"React? Like any other guy who'd just had his brains sucked out via his dick. Like a happy puppy rolling around on the grass."

"Still not seeing the bad here," Anthony prodded kindly. "He enjoyed it and you must have, too, so why the tearful phone call and the late-night visit?"

A kitten meowed as it jumped up between them. "Hey, Raku." Clay extended a hand for the animal to sniff. It hissed at him before drawing back and hiding underneath Anthony's painting stool. "Geez."

"He's temperamental. Probably recognizes the same thing in you, hence the instant dis-like. Raku will come around. The question is, though -- will you?" Anthony took another sip. "You're not answering my questions, Clay. If Seth was happy, and you enjoyed yourself, why the drama?"

"Do you even have to ask? He's straight, Toni. This was just a curiosity thing for him. I might as well have been a hooker he'd paid to scratch his itch. When for me..."

"It meant so much more." Anthony's cup clinked into his saucer. "I'm starting to get the picture now. For you, it was a moment right out of a chick flick. Granted, a chick flick that only me and my ilk would appreciate, but you get the idea. Soaring violin music, fireworks going off overhead, finally getting to taste your one true love..."

"And then realizing it wasn't about what we felt for each other," Clay said softly. "This was just an experiment, and I happened to be con-venient."

Anthony sat in silence for a moment. "Clay?" He looked up at him. "Come over here, would you?"

Frowning, he obeyed. "What's up?"

"Closer." Anthony angled himself with thighs parted, inviting Clay to kneel between them. "Bend your head."

"Anthony, this isn't some kinky -- ow!" He'd smacked Clay. Hard.

Clay reared up, rubbing his smarting scalp. "What the hell did you do that for?"

"Because you're being such a man, you dummy!" Anthony brought his hand down again, this time to help rub away the sting. "You earned that one for acting like a jackass. You left Seth all alone after his first time with a man to come over here and cry on my shoulder?"

"Er…"

"No 'er' about it, mister. You were right -- you did screw up, and big time. What do you think is going on in Seth's head at this moment? Gee, Clay's a pro, he helped me discover something important about myself, hey, wait a second, where did he go?" Anthony pinched one of Clay's ears. "Gay or straight, the Y chromosome doesn't know its ass from its elbow, I swear."

"You think I did the wrong thing by leaving him alone?"

"Think? I *know*." Anthony looked at him with all the sagacity of a yenta who'd spent his life around men, regardless of orientation, which never failed to give Clay a top-grade class of the creeps. No one person under the age of eighty should have Anthony's degree of 'wiser-than-thou' going on. "Clay, what he needed was you by his side, not running away like you hated what you'd done." He paused. "Did you? Hate it, I mean."

"No! God, no. Touching Seth the way I've always wanted to was…" Clay paused, at a loss for words. "Magical. Violins and fireworks, the way you described the moment."

Raku hissed.

"Good boy," Anthony said with a scratch between the furry little ears. "My mother was right. Cats are smarter than men. Who knew? Look, Clay, don't you think Seth felt a little of that enchantment himself? When the afterglow wore off, he probably came looking for you. Wanting to talk about things. And where were you? Burning rubber over here for coffee and comfort. Dummy." His expression softened into a smile. "Clay, honey, you have to go home and sit down with that man."

Clay blanched. "Toni, what the hell do I say? Great sex; now, do you want to talk relationships?"

"Actually, something along those lines, yeah." When Clay groaned and would have turned aside, Anthony caught his chin between two fingers and forced him to look into his eyes. "Oh, no you don't. No running away from this. I've listened to you going on and on about Seth for I don't know how long now. He's been your number one, your big dream. But he was straight, which kept you both safe. Now that he's stepped out of the comfort zone, do you have the guts to follow him?" Anthony shook Clay gently. "Well? Do you?"

Clay gazed up at his best friend, who had his stern face on, mixed with kindly eyes. He sighed. "I'd like to."

"Then go home." Anthony released Clay. "Find that man, and sit him down for a conversation. Talk about all the things that scare you shitless, the both of you. Maybe he's still straight, or maybe he's bi now. Figure out what to do about Sophie beyond making her the butt of a joke. Especially talk about Sophie. I don't trust her. She gives off vibes that make my spine tingle." He looked intently at Clay. "Do we have a deal?"

Clay clenched his fingers, unclenched them, and dipped his head once. "I'll go."

"That's my boy." Anthony rubbed Clay's shoulder briefly, and then the pint-sized powerhouse was on his feet again, dragging Clay up off the ground and giving him a hearty push between the shoulders.

"What are you doing?"

"No time like the present, Clay! You're heading home right now."

"I can't finish my coffee?"

"It's instant. You actually want to drink the whole thing?"

Clay had to concede Anthony's point. Besides, he was starting to get mental visions now. Going home and finding Seth waiting for him in their den. Probably pissed at his having left, but willing to talk things through. Seth, looking good enough to eat in his short blue shorts and his tight T-shirt. Seth, with his soft blond hair and his eyes like the ocean itself.

Seth, the man he loved. The man who might just be interested in loving him back.

"I'm gone," he said, turning just long enough to kiss Anthony on the forehead. "Give me a call tomorrow? I want to let you know how things went."

"I want good news," Anthony informed him seriously. "Make this right, Clay."

"I'll try." Clay squeezed Anthony's hands briefly, then took off out the doorway, down the wooden steps leading up to the studio, and down to his car parked haphazardly across two spaces. Thank God, no one had ticketed or towed it.

All the way home, Clay beat a staccato rhythm on the steering wheel, keeping one eye on the road and focusing all of his mind that he could spare on what he'd say to Seth. Words like *I love you* and *I need you* kept flashing into his head, but he decided it'd be too soon.

We need to talk was where he should start. *This wasn't about curiosity. Not for me, and I*

*don't think it was for you, either. There's some-
thing between us, Seth.*

He imagined himself taking Seth's long,
strong fingers in his own. *Let's figure it out.*

The drive took less time than he would have
thought, but Clay figured he'd just gotten lucky
with traffic. Pulling into his parking space --
neatly, this time -- he bounded up to his door,
thrust the key into his lock, and stepped into…

A dark living room. No Seth in sight.

"Hello?" he called, sensing the utter empti-
ness of the home. "Seth?"

Crossing to the back door, he peered outside. Their blanket still lay on the lawn, in
imminent danger of blowing away with the
winds off the sea, and his bottle of juice, but
no Seth. Clay stared at the spot for a moment,
then ducked back inside. "Seth?"

No one in the kitchen. The bathroom door
stood open, the lights off. That only left…

Clay pulled to a stop in front of Seth's door.
It had been shut tight, but what worried him
more was the note taped to the outside. His
name was scribbled across the front in Seth's
bold, angular handwriting.

He unfolded the missive slowly and read.
When he'd finished, he went back a second
time, just to make sure he hadn't mistaken any
of the words.

No. They were all there in black and white.

Seth didn't want anything more to do with
him.

Slowly, Clay crumpled the note in his fist and dropped it to the floor. Seth could clean up after himself when he got up in the morning, before or after Clay left. Might be early. After all, he'd be looking for a new apartment to move into.

Leaving Seth alone.

Chapter Ten

"Oh, sweetheart," Jeri clucked, rising out of her computer chair. "You look like death warmed over. What on earth happened to you?" She reached for Clay's hands, regardless of her own perfect manicure. "Not only that, you're cold as ice. Honey, what's wrong?"

Clay attempted to summon up a smile. "I'm fine, Jeri. Don't worry."

"Don't worry?" The beautiful trannie made a moue with her carmine lips. "Don't you go telling me such rubbish, now. You're not due into the room for another five, so you sit down and spill the beans. What's got your handsome, happy face turned down like you're heading to a funeral?"

"Yeah, the room… that's kind of what I wanted to talk to you about," Clay hedged. "I don't think I'm up to meeting and greeting today, Jeri. I wanted to get a refund and go home. Can I do that?"

Jeri's plucked eyebrows raised. "Oh, honey, absolutely not. No refunds, or don't you remember that from the waiver you signed? You're down for at least one man today, all paid up."

Clay thought of his nearly-empty wallet and groaned. "Are you sure?"

"Who runs this business, mister, you or me?" Jeri waved a hand dismissively. "Okay, management runs it. But anyone with any common sense knows that the real mover and shaker is their secretary/receptionist. I'm out on the front lines every day, after all. No re- funds, and there are at least two men who are just dying to meet you."

"Yeah. Two men, when I'd rather have just one," Clay muttered. Seth's door had stayed shut all night long -- he'd lain awake in the dark, listening for any sound -- and he hadn't emerged when Clay had come out for coffee and toast, and, at a loss for what to do, taken off for the speed dating agency. He sure as hell didn't want to be there, but where else was he going to go?

His face hardened. Besides, if Seth didn't want him, he'd damn well find someone who did.

"I've changed my mind," he said abruptly. "Let me at 'em."

"Hmm." Jeri put her fingertips together be- neath her chin. "I'd say 'good for you', but something tells me your motives aren't exactly pure. What is it, honey? Man troubles?"

"You'd have to have a man to have troubles with him," Clay said bitterly.

"Oh, no, you don't. I recognize the look on your face now. You've fallen in love with some dashing young stud, and he's blown you off, hasn't he?"

He wasn't exactly the one doing the initial blowing, but -- "Yeah, close enough."

"So? Do you want to tell Jeri all about it? Get things off your chest?"

Clay made a face. "No. God, no. It's a long and messy story, Jeri. I don't want to relive one minute. I need to move on with my life, and I guess that starts with going into this room."

Jeri eyed him for another moment, then rolled her eyes and started typing on a keyboard below the desk. "Room three," she said after a moment. "You paid for one, but there are two men here this morning who want to see you. Do you want to do either/or, or go for both?"

"Both," Clay said recklessly, reaching in his pocket for his last twenty until the next payday. What the hell? He could draw a little against his savings if he needed to, and he could skip lunch. Maybe go for a walk on the beach. Maybe call Jefferson and see if he wanted a run. He had options, didn't he? His happiness didn't depend on whether or not Seth wanted to be a part of his life.

It didn't.

Really.

"Okay, sweet thing." Jeri took the bill and made it disappear with an elegantly practiced movement. "Room three, like I said. Give me a few minutes, and I'll send the first candidate in."

"Sure." Clay paused. "Jeri?"

"Uh-huh, honey?"

"Where do all these guys come from?" Clay gestured to indicate the empty reception area. "I mean, do you have some kind of machine that yanks them through the time/space continuum when they're needed?"

Jeri burst into giggles. "Silly! No, no, no. There's a separate entrance." She pointed to a space behind an overgrown fichus. "That leads to a room where they all wait. And would you believe the number of hookups taking place in that very room?" She clucked her tongue. "Sometimes they don't even make it into the meet and greets."

"My two guys, though?"

"Oh, they're all eager. No straying for them." Jeri clicked a final sequence into her computer. Satisfied, she reached for a key and pressed it into Clay's palm. "Get ready, sugar. Almost showtime. Wash that man right out of your hair, okay?"

"Yeah." Clay grimly tightened his fist around the smooth metal. "That's the plan."

"Go get 'em, tiger!" Jeri cheered him on before turning back to her paperwork. Clay had half an impulse to bend down and kiss her smooth cheek for being such a trouper, but decided against it. She might think he was getting fresh, and he didn't want to be on the receiving end of a redhead's temper tantrum.

Room three was one he hadn't been in before, and Clay thought he liked it. Room one was built on utilitarian lines, without any art or decorations. This felt more like a posh hotel room, with comfortable padded chairs, a nice oriental carpet, and a tapestry hanging on the wall. Some nice potted plants, too. Huh. Maybe they hadn't gotten around to decorating "one" yet -- or maybe Jeri had felt sorry enough for him to give Clay the deluxe accommodations.

Clay sighed, slumping down into the far chair. It sproinged under his weight, molding to his body. He couldn't help making a noise of appreciation. Very, very nice.

Now, all he had to do was wait for Bachelor Number One. God. He shook his head at the patheticness of it all. If he just hadn't blown things with Seth, no pun intended, he might have been waking up to a breakfast with the man. There could have been embarrassed looks followed by grins and laughter, easygoing teasing, and plans for the day. Talks about relationships. Instead, here he was, and who knew where Seth would be heading?

A soft knock sounded at the door. Clay tilted his head in interest. "Well, that's new," he muttered. Then, louder -- "Come in!"

The door slid open, and a tall, thin man slipped inside. Clay blinked. Whoever this was, he had to be at least twenty years older than himself. Not bad-looking, though, not at all. All the same… "I think you might have made a mistake," he said kindly as he could. "I'm Clay. Were you looking for someone else?"

"No, this is the right room. Clay is the man I've come to meet." The man flashed him a half-apologetic smile, then indicated the chair. "May I?"

Clay felt confused, but nodded. "Please."

"Thank you." The man sat with the grace of one who'd long ago learned how to manipulate his body. "My name is James. It's a pleasure to meet you."

He held out a hand to shake. Clay accepted it, surprised in a good way at the lean firmness and the calloused fingertips. "You play an instrument, don't you?" he asked as they sat back. "Guitar?"

"I dabble a little," James admitted. He let his hands fall loosely onto the arms of the chair, and fidgeted. "I don't find it surprising that you were startled to see me here. I am old enough to be your father, after all."

"Oh, no, no," Clay hastened.

James waved him off. "I can tell a lie from the truth, no matter how well-intentioned." He smiled wearily. "It was your eyes, you see. I saw your photograph and knew I had to meet the man with so much good humor that it spilled over into a stock picture. I find myself..." He picked at the chair arm. "In need of a laugh or two."

Clay examined James again, more carefully this time. He had the air of a man who'd been through some serious valleys, and recently, too. The look was one he recognized. A switch flipped in his brain and he leaned forward. "Your lover left you, didn't he?"

James' head came up. "How did you -- oh, I suppose it's written all over my face, isn't it?" He sighed. "Yes, you're right. My partner of twenty years has moved out. The place is so empty that I don't know what to do with myself."

"What happened?"

"What didn't?" James sighed. "A partnership is much like a marriage. Exactly like, in a number of ways. It fell apart the way things usually do. Small spats turn into week-long arguments, nothing you do is good enough, you're taking too many risks, you're too careful, and before you know it the final straw has snapped and you're on your own."

Clay made a sympathetic noise. "Rough, my friend. So what was that last straw?"

James looked embarrassed. "I bought a motorcycle. My lover, Stuart, wouldn't hear of me riding it, especially at my age. He thought it was far too dangerous."

"Those choppers are pretty hard to handle." Clay thought, for a moment, of Seth on his own bike. He didn't know how Seth managed to rope and ride that beast of his, but he did it with such ease that it seemed like second nature. All the same, he worried about the man every time he peeled out of the driveway. Cycles were damned dangerous, and no mistake about it.

Realizing that James was speaking, Clay dragged his attention back to the present moment. "He said this was the end." James dragged a hand through his hair, shot through with silver. "Said that I was trying to recapture my youth, and if I wasn't contented by growing old with him, I'd better go find someone more my mental age to spend time with. Then he packed up, and he was gone."

Clay felt a twinge of sympathy. "But you miss him, don't you?" he asked. "Like there's a hole in your chest where he ought to fit."

"How did you know?" James gave Clay a puzzled look. "Aren't you too young to have gone through this?"

"What's age matter? I know a few things about having a heart broken." Clay reached out impulsively and took James' hand again. "What did you do about the bike?"

James half-laughed. "I sold it as soon as I could find a buyer."

"Did you tell Stuart?"

"I tried, but he's been blocking my calls."

"Harsh. Have you tried going to see him in person?"

"Time after time." James looked despondent. "Listen to me, going on and on about the man I love when I'm supposed to be getting to know you."

Clay grinned. "James, you didn't come here for a date. You didn't pick me out because I was cute. You wanted a listening ear. You've got it, and you've also got a quick fix." He pulled out his cell phone. Finger on the CALL button, he paused to ask -- "You're sure you want him back?"

"More than anything. It isn't that you're not a charming young man, but you are right," James admitted. "Coming here was a crazy idea, but what else could I do? I felt that if there was no way to get Stuart back, I had to get over him."

"Nope. No way." Clay punched the button. "You lucked out today, friend. Give me his number." He punched in the digits as James rattled them off. Putting a finger to his lips, he summoned up his best DJ voice.

"Hello?" a voice answered. Older, tired and sad. "Stuart here."

"And there's our lucky winner!" Clay exclaimed, making a few whistling noises.

"What? Who is this?"

"Welcome to WKZL, Stuart. This is Clay, filling in for the regular DJ. Today we're playing a little game with the White Pages. I've been going through at random and handing out deluxe dinners for two at the best restaurant in town, the Swordfish Plaza. You're the first one to answer his phone, so you're our lucky winner!"

"Oh!" Stuart sounded a little better now. Pleased. "That's wonderful news. But..." he trailed off. "For two? I don't -- I mean -- it's only me."

"A guy like you doesn't have anyone he can call to spend a night eating the best seafood this town has to offer? Oh, come on, now," Clay teased. "What about old friends? Anyone you have unfinished business with?"

Stuart was silent for a long minute. "I have a friend," he admitted in a low voice. "We parted... not on the best of terms."

"Well, here's your chance to bridge the gap. Give him a call. Who knows? Maybe you can do some quality bonding over a plate of grilled red snapper. And let me tell you, they do it right over there." Clay made a kissing noise. "Spices like you wouldn't believe."

"Maybe," Stuart said. "I have to think about it."

"You do that, sir. Congratulations on winning your prize, and you have a good evening tonight. Just tell the hostess that Clay sent you, and she'll get you taken care of."

"Thank you." Stuart's voice was shaking.

"It's no trouble at all." Clay gave a chuckle. "Thanks for listening to WKZL, my man. You have a good day now!"

He disconnected. James was staring at him in amazement. "What... what on God's green earth did you just do?"

Clay grinned. "Got you two on the path back together, is what I did."

"But -- how?"

"Look." Clay took James' hands again. "There's a whole world of possibilities. Stuart might give you a call, or he might not. If he does, great! Go there and let him know how much you miss him, and how desperately you want a second chance. Twenty years is a long time to just up and end it all. You need one more shot to work things out."

"And if he doesn't call?"

"You're still covered. Go to the restaurant yourself, tonight. Ten'll get you twenty that Stuart shows up alone. Do you know of anyone else he might invite?"

James slowly shook his head. "No. Stuart and I had plenty of acquaintances, but they were all couples, like ourselves. There isn't anyone single he might invite, unless he's met someone..."

"Never happen. Not the way he sounded. That was the voice of a man who's still way down deep in the dumps over what's happened between you two. If you have to go by yourself, you'll see him sitting alone at a table. You go over and join him. No way he'll make a scene in a place like the Swordfish. The two of you get a chance to talk, and you tell him everything you've told me. You want another chance. He could say yes, he could say no, but at least you'll know. Isn't that better than what you came in here for?"

James broke into a grin. He gripped Clay's hands back, shaking them. "Thank you, young man. Thank you. And hold on... you really are a DJ, aren't you? I think I've heard you before."

"WKZL," Clay said with an answering smile. "We have boatloads of free passes to restaurants. Just swing by the office this afternoon and say Clay sent you. Get to the Swordfish early and slip the hostess those comps. Everything's going to be taken care of."

James looked moved. "You are a remarkable man, Clay. I knew, when I saw your eyes..." He had to stop to clear his throat. "I can't thank you enough."

"I don't need thanks. Now get out of here, would you?" Clay let go of the strong older hands. "Go pick out what you're going to wear tonight."

James' eyes sparkled. "Stuart's favorite suit. I have one he always loved to see on me."

"Well, there you go! Now scoot. Go get that man, tiger."

James stood, flashing a brilliant smile back at Clay. "Remarkable," he murmured, and then, "Thank you. From the bottom of my heart."

Clay raised a hand in the air and pumped it. "You go, friend."

When the door closed behind him, Clay leaned back in the chair, taking a deep breath. That had felt cleansing, somehow. Maybe he couldn't fix his problems with Seth, but he could still help someone else.

"You really are the last of the romantics," Jeri's voice piped through the intercom.

Clay laughed, not really surprised at the interruption. "You sneak. You were listening to the whole thing, weren't you?"

"Only a little…"

"Oh, give it up."

"All right, I heard the whole thing. I've never seen a man more hangdog than this poor James character, and the look on his face when he saw your picture? I had to get an earful. Don't be mad?"

"Not mad, Jeri, don't worry." Clay petted the intercom box as fondly as if it were her shoulder. "Talk about a love story, huh?"

"Oh, yeah," Jeri breathed happily. "Do you think they'll get back together?"

Clay thought about the sadness in Stuart's voice and the matching sorrow on James' face. "I think maybe so, yeah," he mused. "If nothing else, they'll find some kind of closure."

"James was right, you know," Jeri said. "You are a good man."

"Oh, bah." Clay waved that aside. "I'm just someone who helps out every now and then. So, you got another one for me? Is he ready?"

"Primed like a gun."

"This isn't one of those scary guys like Michael, is it?" Clay stiffened. "I don't think I can handle another punk."

"Definitely not a punk, sugar. In fact, if I thought he went in for my type, I'd have claimed him for myself." Jeri made an *mmm-mmm* noise. "This one is fine as wine, darling. Cute as a button and dressed so sharp I could cut myself. Do you want me to give him the go-ahead?"

Clay felt a shudder of anticipation, which startled him. Maybe it was the leftover thrill from helping James and Stuart, he rationalized. "Yeah, Jeri. Send him in."

Waiting, Clay idly swung his foot back and forth. Something white flashed, and he realized that one shoelace had come untied. With a noise of impatience, he bent down to fix it, grumbling under his breath about stupid trainers and not being in kindergarten all over again. The chair, which had seemed sturdy enough, suddenly tipped forward, landing Clay on his forearms with a painful crunch, his ass in the air.

"Well, I had planned on a handshake," a warm voice, rich as brandy wine, said with some amusement. "But then again, this isn't such a bad way to say hello either."

Clay felt his cheeks turn bright red. *Figures.* He righted himself, pushing the chair back into position before tossing hair out of his eyes and standing up to greet the new entrant.

He went from red to pale in a heartbeat. "Seth?" he asked, his lips going numb.

The newcomer cocked his head. "Who? No, sorry. My name's Taylor. Do I remind you of someone you know?"

"A little, yeah." Clay sank down in the treacherous chair, staring for all he was worth. God almighty, this Taylor could be Seth's twin. The same wavy blond hair, the same angled face, the same sparkling eyes. But the closer he looked, the more differences he could see. Taylor stood a couple of inches shorter, his clothes were the latest out of that trendy cata-logue, and his lips were a bit thinner.

"Do you mind if I have a seat, or should I stand here for a while longer?" Taylor teased.

Clay took a deep breath. Even the voices were close to alike. "You don't have a brother, or a cousin…?" he ventured. "Someone who lives around here?"

"Sorry, no. I moved into town last month."

"Small world," Clay muttered. "You know, there's a guy in town who could be your twin."

"Really? Is he charming, sexy, and witty?" Taylor winked. "Can I give him a run for his money?"

To his own surprise, Clay chuckled. Taylor sat down, easily crossing his legs at the knee. He held out a hand. "Pleased to meet you."

Clay took the strong fingers in his own, and felt a slight shock of electricity. Chemistry. "Good to meet you," he said, a little awed. "So you are new in town? And this is how you meet people?"

Taylor gave an easy shrug. "It's a lot quicker than meat markets," he said, tilting his head exactly the way Seth did when he was amused. "Better choice, too. Besides, I'd never tried anything like this operation. I thought it would be fun. How long have you been up on the block?"

"Few days now."

"And no one's snapped you up?"

"Not yet," Clay admitted.

"More fools them." Taylor gave Clay a quizzical look. "Why?"

Clay felt his cheeks coloring again. "That's kind of a long story…"

"Would you like to discuss it over dinner?"

That brought Clay sharply back to attention. "You're asking me out?"

"Why not? I've been around a few days myself, and I've never seen anyone who appealed to me like you. I want to get to know this Clay better." Taylor smiled. "From the look on your face, you're either horrified or delighted."

"I'm not sure," Clay answered honestly. His brain felt like a tilt-a-whirl. This man could have been Seth, except for the open and frankly gay attitude. Would it be accepting an imitation designer original, or finding a steal? He truly couldn't tell. "Can I have a minute to think about it?"

Taylor made an expansive gesture. "All the time you need. I'm not going anywhere." He cast an eye to the timer and cracked another grin. "At least not until that buzzes, at any rate."

Clay managed to return his look of good humor before returning to his thoughts. *Not Seth, not Seth, not Seth,* part of his brain chanted before another part chimed in with *Seth rejected you. This man just happens to look like him. Does that mean you should say no? Of course not, dummy! He's a prize, and he's interested in you. What were you saying earlier? Go get 'im!*

"If it helps, I'm not after your masculine virtue," Taylor teased. "I'm just one of the last true romantics. All I had in mind was a dinner at a good restaurant --"

"Not seafood," Clay said absently.

"A steak house, then. We can share a good bottle of wine, then go for a walk on the shore. Corny as it might sound, there are those of us who appreciate a stroll along the sands." Taylor's eyes were twinkling. "I'll keep my shoes on, though, thanks."

"Jellyfish," they said together.

Clay couldn't help it -- he cracked up. "You make a pretty convincing argument," he relented. "You want me to be straight with you?"

"Well, no. I'd rather you were gay, or this whole arrangement is pretty pointless, wouldn't you agree?" Taylor's eyes twinkled as Clay had to laugh. "But if you're asking me if I'd like you to be honest? Then the answer is yes. I can tell there's something holding you back, and I'd like to know what it is. Would it have anything to do with this man I resemble?"

"More than less," Clay admitted. "Except he is straight, as in the non-homosexual meaning of the word. My housemate. We were really good friends."

"Were? As in the past tense?"

"I'm thinking very past, now."

"There was an argument? A fight?"

"Suffice it to say I screwed up big time, and now he wants me to move out." Clay stared down at his lap, watching his hands curl into fists. He unclenched them with an effort. "The guy meant -- means -- a lot to me. I don't know what I'm going to do without him."

Taylor looked thoughtful. "You had a crush on him, didn't you?"

Clay winced.

"Thought so." Taylor reached out and placed a hand on Clay's knee. Rather than an intrusion, it felt like a simple dose of comfort. Nothing sexual about the move. Just comfort. "I've been there myself, you know. Trouble is, nothing down that road but tears. There's no use wasting our time mooning over people who don't want us back, at least not in the way we'd like."

Clay nodded grudgingly. He couldn't tell Taylor about the whole gay-joke thing, much less about the blow job in his backyard. Some things weren't meant to be shared, and he had the feeling Seth would really blow his stack if he ever found out.

He looked up at Taylor, taking in every detail of the man. So close to the way Seth looked, from the tips of his hair down to his long, narrow feet. Kind. Understanding. And gay, or at least he said so. Here to meet another man he'd like to spend time with. The perfect guy, or at least he should have been.

Clay spared a thought for Michael, Adam, and Jefferson. What had been wrong with him? Michael aside as a definite "some night when I'm desperate", they had been guys he could have hooked up with. Why hadn't he? Easy answer -- a terminal case of Seth on the brain.

Maybe it was time he took Jeri's advice, and come to it, Taylor's too. Time to get over himself and move forward. Yeah. He could. He should.

Any minute now, he would.

"Aw, God," he burst out. "I can't."

Taylor blinked. "You what, now?"

"I'm sorry, and I know this sounds like a bad line, but it's not you. It's me."

"Clay." Taylor tented his fingers. "You can't keep mooning after this guy. Not when there's a whole big world of gay men out there just looking for someone as special as you."

"I know, I know." Clay made a fist and struck his own knee. "Look, under any other circumstances, I would have jumped at you. And I do mean jumped. We'd be on the floor already with my tongue in your ear."

Taylor laughed. A good sign. "Maybe something a little less sloppy?"

"I'm flexible. Point is..." Clay spread his hands. "I'm just not over this guy yet. I don't know how long it'll take until I will be. But before that day comes, I couldn't give anyone I dated anything but second-best."

"I see." Taylor sighed. "No, no, I do understand. The heart loves where it will, right? But you keep my number. Maybe in a few days, a week, a month, when your head's cleared up, give me a call. Even if I'm with someone by then, we can still go out for a few drinks."

Clay felt about two inches tall. "You're a better man than I am," he said frankly. "I'd have been out that door already."

"Ah, I don't think you give yourself enough credit." Taylor bent and gave Clay a soft kiss on the top of his head. "You take care, now, you hear?"

Clay nodded, taking Taylor's hand in a lingering grasp as he turned to walk out of the door. "I'm sorry," he offered.

Taylor paused, hand on the knob. "Yeah. Me, too." Then, he smiled. "Maybe we'll meet again. Some other time, some other place."

"If I can, I will," Clay answered him as honestly as he could, although he couldn't see himself getting over Seth anytime soon.

And with that, Taylor was gone. Clay groaned and flung himself into the chair, pounding the armrests. "I am such a moron!" he accused himself. "A fine guy like Taylor, and I let him get away? Jesus, what's wrong with me?"

"Maybe there's someone you can't get out of your mind," a familiar voice said.

Jeri cut in on the intercom. "Clay, there's a guy headed your way. I couldn't stop him. He said he knew you, and you wouldn't be mad."

Clay didn't look up. "Jeri?"

"Yeah, sweetie?"

"Would this be the guy who came with me on my first speed date?"

"That's the one."

Clay switched off the intercom. He looked up. At Seth. Not an imitation, but the real thing. Somewhat the worse for wear, looking like he'd had a sleepless night, with his hair sticking up in seven different directions and dark circles under his eyes, but… Seth.

"What are you doing here?" Clay asked through numb lips.

Seth leaned on the back of the empty chair. "Looking for you," he said with a faint trace of good humor. "As for why, that's another question."

"Why, then?" Clay's heart began to beat trip-hammer fast in his chest.

"Because of last night. Because I couldn't forget you. Me. What we did." Seth looked into Clay's eyes and refused to let him break the contact. "What I did."

"What you did," Clay repeated dumbly. "The note."

"Yeah." Seth dragged a hand through his disheveled hair. "Clay, we have to talk."

Clay nodded silently.

"Can I have a seat?"

"Please." Clay watched as the man he loved with all his might came around to sit casually in his chair. He couldn't take his eyes off the guy. His throat felt thick, as if he were trying to swallow down some huge lump of emotion. "Seth, why are you here?"

Seth flashed Clay a look he couldn't interpret. "To take my shot at charming you into a date," he said.

To which Clay could find nothing to say at all. Not one single word.

Until his mouth opened, and out fell -- "Holy *shit.*"

Chapter Eleven

Seth's mouth crooked up at one corner. "Yeah. Pretty much what I was thinking all the way over here. Speaking of which, way to treat a guy like dog crap last night, huh?"

"Seth, I am so sorry. You have no idea how --"

"No, I don't. I didn't, either." Seth rubbed at his cheeks, making a sandpapery sound. "Do you really not know what all that in the yard was about?"

Clay felt as if he were lost at sea. "You were… curious," he fumbled. "Looking for someone to show you what it was all about."

Seth gave him a long, level look. "And that's it?"

"Pretty much. Seth, what do you want to say?"

"How about you start with the truth?"

"Clay, is everything okay in there?" Jeri called through the door. "I have a hot button to the police if you're in trouble, so don't you even think about starting anything, whoever you are!"

"Easy. I've got a problem with him, but we're not about to start hitting each other." Seth glanced at Clay. "Are we?"

Clay shook his head. "We're clear, Jeri."

"If you say so." She sounded doubtful. "But if I hear one raised word or a single thing go *crash,* I'm on the phone to my buddies in the force."

"Geez," Seth mumbled. "Wonder if they're my buddies, too. Wouldn't that figure?"

Clay struggled for a grip on the moment. "Seth, focus. I thought, last night, you were all about exploring sex with a man. It didn't matter which man. I was there, and you trusted me. When it was over, I... I..." He fell silent. "I couldn't handle things, okay? I went over to Anthony's."

"Leaving me out in the backyard, floating on the best orgasm of my life, wondering when you'd come back." Seth's voice dropped. "I had my hands on myself, Clay. Wishing you'd hurry up with whatever you were doing and get outside with me again, where you belonged."

Clay shook his head. "Seth, don't read more into this than need be. What we shared, it wasn't --"

"Oh, no, you don't." Seth held up a finger. "You don't get to say it wasn't special. And since when do you have the right to make up my mind for me? Clay, you need to sit there and listen, because I have a few things to say. Can you promise me you'll just be quiet until I have this all off my chest?"

Clay nodded hesitantly, not opening his mouth.

"Good." Seth got up and began to pace the room, punctuating his words with choppy hand gestures. "When you didn't come back last night, I got myself dressed and went inside. I looked for you everywhere, in each room, and then I thought to check for your car. Gone. You know how seeing an empty spot in the driveway made me feel? I had no idea why you'd left. In my head, I was thinking you'd taken off because you couldn't stand to look at me.

"Hence, the note." Seth took in a deep breath. "I heard you come home and take it off the door, but damn it, Clay, I was so mad at you by then I couldn't think straight. I figured you'd been off somewhere washing the taste of me out of your mouth."

"Seth, no, I didn't --"

"I know, I know. Anthony's, like you said. But if you were me, and the guy who'd just had sex with you fled like a bat out of hell, what would you think? And don't you start with the 'but you're straight' line. I'm starting to think maybe I'm not, Clay. I'm open to new things."

His voice softened. "I'd been hoping you would come back and open my eyes to a few more," he said. "But no Clay, no further adventures, and I got madder and madder. But then, as I lay awake, I started to think. Anthony's got

his nose into everything, you know? He figured it out long before I did."

Clay couldn't hold back the words. "What
did he know?"

Seth barked a laugh. "That I loved you,
dumbass. There. I said it. I don't know when it
started, or why, but after last night, I was sure.
And I was just as sure that I hated you, too.

"I slept maybe an hour. Thinking about you,
the night we went to that bar and got drunk. I
tucked you in and I couldn't drop off as long as
I was by your side. Just being near you made
me question too many things about myself."

"Anthony knew?"

"That man is way too smart for his own
good," Seth grumbled. "He told me I had to
make up my own mind, but you did that for
me. I didn't want to, you understand that? I
wanted to play this game out, and go back to
chasing skirts. But you -- you got inside my
heart somehow, and I couldn't get you out
again. I didn't want to. And that's what I realized last night.

"Fell asleep around dawn. When I woke up,
you were gone again, and I knew there was
only one place you could have gone. I didn't
stop to think, to get dressed, hell, even to comb
my hair. The only thing that mattered was getting to you before someone else swept you
up."

Seth sank to one knee in front of Clay's
chair. "I'm scared, okay? I don't understand

any of this. Why you, why me. All I know is that it exists. The big elephant in the room. We can dance around it, but we can't pretend it doesn't exist."

"Seth…"

"Stop interrupting. Please. Clay, I want you. I need you. I have no idea where this is heading, but I want you along for the ride. Can you handle a passenger in the car? I need to know the answer, man. Are you willing to guide me through whatever's on the way, guide me over the speed bumps, help me understand myself?" He reached up to touch Clay's face with a surprisingly gentle hand. "Please, Clay. I'm scared, and you're the only anchor I can hang onto right now." His voice dropped to a bare whisper. "I love you."

Something broke in Clay's heart. Once, when he was a kid, he'd read a story about a man who had three iron bands around his heart. When his dreams came true, the bands shattered for joy. He could live again, breathe deep, and he could love. Staring down at Seth, Clay suddenly understood that fairy-tale man. He drew in a breath, and it tasted fresh.

Slowly, he raised his hand to Seth's, covering it with his fingers. "I've ached for you for so long," he admitted. "Probably from the first moment I saw you. You're damned good-looking, you know that?"

The two shared a laugh. "It's not on purpose," Seth offered.

"Dumbass. I know. It was lust at first sight, sure, but you were straight. Shut up. You *were*, back then. I didn't have any idea this might happen. So I got to know you better, and the more I learned about you, the more I liked what I found. You're a fine cop, a good man, and a great friend. I watched you day after day, and none of the men I dated once or twice even came close to measuring up. You were the yardstick, Seth." Clay shook his head. "I couldn't believe it when you let me touch you… all the way. I thought I'd explode, but I thought for sure you didn't care about me in that way. I was just an experiment. I couldn't stand that when I loved you as much as I did. So I ran."

Seth shut his eyes tightly. After a moment, he shook his head. "We are two messed up fellas, aren't we?" he asked ruefully.

"You could say that." On impulse, Clay slipped off the chair and down onto his knees beside Seth. "So, we've got the basics covered. You're the ship, and I'm the anchor. You're hanging on and I'm full speed ahead."

Seth's cheeks pinked. "More or less. That is, if you're willing."

"I don't think willing is a strong enough word." Clay pressed in closer, gripping Seth's hands in his own. "More like jumping up and down and screaming *yes*!"

Seth laughed brokenly. "I kept going over and over things in my mind, right? The stuff we have scattered around the house. That broken conch shell we played football with. Your bottles of every-flavor juice that crowded out my plain old O.J. The way you always told me to wear my helmet." He squeezed Clay's hands. "How relieved you looked every single time I came home. And then I realized, we were home. Both of us together. We were what made that house a home. It's a cliché, but it's true."

"Like we belong together," Clay said quietly. "It's how I've always felt, too. Leave it to Anthony to figure out the real skinny before either of us did."

"Nothing like a woman." Seth sighed and leaned in so that his forehead touched Clay's. "It was the dumbest idea I've ever come up with, trying to convince Sophie I was gay, but on the other hand, it was the greatest stroke of luck ever. Better than Babe Ruth on a winning streak."

"You're mixing your metaphors."

"Isn't that allowed when you're spilling your heart?"

"I'll let it slide." Clay pressed his lips to Seth's forehead. Chaste, easy, slow. "What about this? Can you let this slide?"

Seth's hands tightened around Clay's. "No," he said hoarsely. "Not when I want to come along for the ride. And I do, Clay. I swear, I do."

"Then follow my lead. Close your eyes." As soon as the lashes fluttered shut, Clay began laying kisses over the whole of Seth's face. Forehead, cheekbones, the tip of his nose, and, ever so lightly, over each closed eyelid. Finally, he reached Seth's mouth, and spoke, knowing that his breath would tickle -- "And here? Can I kiss you here?"

"God, but I wish you would," Seth whispered.

When their lips touched, Clay almost heard the violins begin to play and the fireworks go off overhead. "That's good," he said, short of breath, "but this is the way real men do it." He freed his hands from Seth's and reached up to tangle them in the man's hair.

His kiss turned from gentle to bruising, thrusting his tongue into a mouth that opened wide and willing for him. Two tongues wrapped around each other in a rough dance, thrusting at one another without any need to go easy to coax the other into playing. Clay nibbled at Seth's bottom lip, then soothed away the sting, and dived back in.

When he pulled away for air, Seth's eyes were dazed. "Wow," he said faintly. "So that's what it's all about."

"And more." Clay would have dived back in for a second kiss, but once again, Seth surprised him.

Loosening one of Clay's hands, Seth brought it down to touch his groin. Clay's lips parted at the feel of the hard erection underneath Seth's pants, straining upward at his zipper. "Seth?"

Seth looked at him with confusion. "Is it normal?" he asked. "To get this horny off just one kiss?"

Clay had to laugh. "Call it a good sign that you're where you want to be."

"This isn't where I want to be." Seth licked his lips, closing his eyes halfway. "I'd like to be back in the yard, on that blanket, listening to the waves and the seagulls. Feeling you beside me. Showing me things I may have heard of, but never felt."

"Nothing's stopping us from going home now," Clay whispered. "We can get up and drive there right this second."

Seth started to open his mouth, then closed it. He shook his head. "No. First, I have to get one thing straightened out."

"What could you possibly --"

"Sophie."

Clay sat back, stunned. "What?"

"I owe her an explanation. An apology. Something. She might have been a bitch, Clay, but we were together for months. She needs to know the truth about me, and why I really have changed now."

Clay sighed. "Damn your sense of honor."

"It always has gotten me into trouble." Shyly, Seth nuzzled at Clay's face. "Can I try what you just did sometime?"

"Go ahead now, if you want." Clay shut his eyes. There was a moment's pause, and then, spurring a burst in his heartbeat, he felt Seth's lips on his face. Light brushes over his face, somehow better than the rough kiss they'd shared. This was Seth, giving of himself for Clay's own pleasure. Freely, no pushing or shoving.

Finally, the lips came back down to rest on Clay's, and Clay wasn't able to hold it in any longer. Grabbing Seth around the middle, he tackled him down to the floor, careful not to make any noise. One hand snaked down between them and gripped Seth's hard-on. Seth made a strangled noise and bucked up, filling Clay's palm with the feel of solid male flesh.

"It gets better," Clay whispered. "Remember what I did last night?"

Seth blinked hazily. "You mean -- right here?"

"Not a blow job. Something else. Do you trust me?"

Seth gazed at Clay for a long moment. Finally, he nodded.

"Help me with these," Clay instructed, his fingers going to the snap and zip on Seth's jeans. Together, they pulled the restrictive garment down to his knees, and then the tight gray jockey shorts. Clay breathed in for a moment, savoring the raw smell of pure man. He reached to take the tempting column of flesh in his own hand --

But Seth stopped him. "Not only for me," he whispered. "I can see you, Clay. I can almost smell you. I don't want this to be a one-way street."

A thrill of excitement coursed through Clay's veins. "There is something different I can show you," he said. "Think you can be quiet?"

Seth nodded.

"Then help me with my own jeans." Clay's hands were shaking almost too hard to manipulate the fabric. Seth wasn't much better off, but between the two of them, they managed to get all obstacles out of the way.

Once he was bare, Seth stared. Clay let him, knowing that this was, again, something entirely new to Seth. One forefinger stole out to touch. When flesh made contact, Clay hissed.

Seth jerked back. "Jesus! Did I scratch you?"

Clay laughed. "No way, moron. I say that with love. You're doing just what I like best -- well, almost best. There is absolutely no wrong here. Go ahead and touch me. Feel me. Look at me. It's all right. I promise you."

Slow and cautious, Seth reached out to cup Clay's cock in his hand. He ran his fingers lightly up and down the shaft, tracing each vein and circling around the mushroom head. "It's different," he said at last, voice shaking. "Not like mine at all. I mean, I've seen others -- locker rooms, showers -- but never one up close. In my hand." Clay saw him struggle to get a grip on the moment. "I didn't imagine I'd ever hold one."

"Hush," Clay soothed. "No talking. No thinking, unless you're doubting yourself."

"I'm not."

"Then just let it go," Clay encouraged. "Let yourself feel all you want. Or," he said, carefully unwrapping Seth's hand, "we can do this."

"What are you…"

"Ssh. Watch. And feel. Above all else, feel." Steadying his hands, Clay brought their two erections into contact, and then laid his hands on top of both, holding them together.

"Oh, God!"

"Quiet! Jeri's going to wonder what's going on." Clay reached over to kiss Seth's lips briefly. "No thoughts, now. Just feel."

And with that, he began to stroke their cocks together, rough and hard. The way a man liked it, quick and harsh. Seth strangled a cry by biting at his forearm, and the sight of him, caught in a passion he was only beginning to understand, was almost enough to drive Clay over the edge.

"It gets better," he encouraged, picking up the speed of his stroke. He paused to slick his hands with the pre-come dripping from both of their cocks. "Like this. Feel?"

Seth nodded, then threw his head back, eyes shut tight. "Close," he managed to say. "Way too close. It's the way you feel, Clay. You're making me crazy."

Clay laughed through his shortness of breath. "That's the way it should be." Releasing his grip, he dove down and sucked Seth's cock into his mouth. He rode the movement as Seth gasped and fell backwards on his ass, following through, never losing contact. When Seth was stable again, he slid as much of the shaft down his throat as he could, then drew back up slowly, applying the suction he knew felt so very good.

"Clay," Seth whispered raggedly, "Gonna. Gonna come. Can't wait."

It's okay, Clay told him silently, and lashed the head of Seth's cock with his tongue. He felt Seth's balls draw up tight, and then, at last, his mouth filled with salty fluid. Lapping up each drop, swallowing it down with absolute pleasure, he ignored his own hard-on for the pleasure of tasting Seth.

As he had the night before, Seth hung limp for a moment, then shook his head. "You, now. I want you."

"It's too soon, Seth…"

"Just a taste." Seth was gathering his legs beneath him, shining cock hanging between his legs. The sight of it had Clay's pulse racing. Seth licked his lips. "I want to. Please?"

Gently, but with the force of a strong man, Seth pushed Clay over onto his back. Clay went with the motion, too stunned to protest.

Was Seth really doing this? Did he have any clue what he was getting into?

Apparently, he did. Lashing his tongue over his lips one more time, Seth dipped down and pressed a kiss to the tip of Clay's cock. "It tastes different," he whispered. "Strange, but good. Like you smell, only stronger."

"It gets better," Clay managed.

"Kind of a novice at this," Seth warned.

"Like I said before? There is no wrong here." Clay reached for Seth, only managing to brush his skin. "Just do what feels natural. But do it fast, will you? I'm this close to coming, and you're just -- God, you're just --"

Seth took pity on Clay by moving. Slowly, he slid his mouth over the head of Clay's cock, his tongue taking curious swipes. Clay groaned and flung an arm over his eyes.

For someone who didn't have much practice, Seth seemed to have natural talent. He found exactly the right places to put his hands, where to squeeze, and where to stroke. Clay felt his balls being rolled in Seth's palms, and almost lost it then and there.

"My turn to warn you," he gasped. "Don't swallow if you don't want. It's okay."

Seth shook his head gently, sucking hard. His cheeks hollowed out. He wanted this, Clay could tell.

"Seth --" he managed to choke out before his own orgasm fell on him like a ravening tiger, clawing its way out from the pit of his stomach and roaring out of his cock. He came with such force that he was afraid Seth would choke, but although he looked startled, Seth swallowed like a man. Dribbles escaped his lips, and he chased after them as Clay spurted into his mouth, down his throat, across his mouth.

When it was over, Clay felt boneless and limp as he ever had. Seth pulled off and sat above him, staring down with worried eyes. "Did I -- I mean, was that okay?"

"Okay?" Clay croaked. "Any better, and you'd have killed me. Come here." He held one arm open for Seth. Seth crawled down into the grip with only a little awkwardness.

"I didn't know how much guys could like to do this," he confessed.

"You have a lot to learn," Clay said into Seth's hair. "It's okay, though. I'm here for the ride. Anchors aweigh, remember?"

Seth laughed. "This is... nice," he said. "I never thought, you know? But it's good."

"Then just enjoy it." Clay paused. "Until Jeri kicks us out, that is."

"Let's not give her a chance to." Seth sat up, offering Clay his hand. "Let's go home. What do you say? You and me, back at the place where all this started. It's our place. Let's christen it the way it should be."

Clay let himself be pulled up. Seizing Seth by the shoulders, he gave the man a long kiss.

"Sounds perfect to me," he murmured.
"Clothes, and then home."

Seth gave him a sideways looks. "Is right about now when one of us is supposed to say, 'this looks like the beginning of a beautiful friendship'?"

Clay considered the question. "Probably. Do you think it applies?"

"I'm pretty sure it does." Seth's smile was bright as his eyes. "Come on, big guy. I want to get out of here."

"Ready to face whatever comes next?"

"Ready, willing, and able." Seth took a deep breath. "As long as you're there, I can handle this."

"And I'm not going anywhere." Clay stroked Seth's arm. "We're in this together. And we can both deal with Sophie."

He held out his hand. "Partners?"

Seth gave him the look that Clay had fallen in love with months ago. He shook Clay's hand. "Partners."

And together, Clay knew they could face whatever the world threw at them.

Enjoyed The Name of the Game?

Look for Willa Okati's newest novel, Faire Grounds, coming from Torquere Press in August 2007!

http://www.torquerepress.com

LaVergne, TN USA
13 September 2010
196798LV00004B/7/A